Praise for Jorn Lier Horst's *William Wisting* series

'Horst, a former Norwegian policeman, now produces classy procedurals with plotting, depth and humanity to rival the best of the Scandis.'   -*The Sunday Times* Crime Club

'Urban rather than natural settings are the stamping grounds of Jorn Lier Horst, whose *Dregs* is immensely impressive. The writer's career as a police chief has supplied a key ingredient for the crime fiction form: credibility.'

    -Barry Forshaw, author of *Nordic Noir* and *Euro Noir*

'*Closed for Winter* is a piece of quality craftsmanship, bringing together an unexpectedly winding plot, highly intelligent characterizations and a delectably subtle noir mood to create a very engrossing crime novel.'   -*Edinburgh Book Review*

'Expertly constructed and beautifully written, [*The Hunting Dogs*] showcases the talents of one of the most accomplished authors of contemporary Nordic Noir.'

                -Karen Meek, The Petrona Award

'*The Caveman* is not just an intriguing, fast-paced thriller, but a thoughtful meditation on loneliness, and a moving testament to the value of human life.'

        -Nicola Upson, author of the *Josephine Tey* series

'Horst writes some of the best Scandinavian crime fiction available. His books are superbly plotted and addictive, the characters superbly realised. *Ordeal* kept me engaged to the end and I cannot wait for the next.'   -Yrsa Sigurdardottir

Jorn Lier Horst is one of Scandinavia's most successful crime writers. For many years he was one of Norway's most experienced police officers, with the result that his engaging and intelligent novels offer a realistic insight into how serious crimes are investigated, and how they are handled by the media. The critically acclaimed William Wisting Series has sold more than one million copies in Norway, and is translated into thirty languages. Jorn's literary awards include the Norwegian Booksellers' Prize, the Riverton Prize (Golden Revolver), the Scandinavian Glass Key and the prestigious Martin Beck Award; *The Caveman* won the United Kingdom's Petrona Award in 2016.

Anne Bruce lives on the Isle of Arran in Scotland and studied Norwegian and English at Glasgow University. She is the translator of Jorn Lier Horst's *Dregs, Closed for Winter, The Hunting Dogs, The Caveman* and *Ordeal,* and also Anne Holt's *Blessed are Those who Thirst* (2012), *Death of the Demon* (2013), *The Lion's Mouth* (2014), *Dead Joker* (2015), *No Echo* (2016), *Beyond the Truth* (2016) and *What Dark Clouds Hide* (2017), in addition to Merethe Lindstrøm's Nordic Prize winning *Days in the History of Silence* (2013).

The William Wisting Series
Published in English by Sandstone Press

Dregs
Closed for Winter
The Hunting Dogs
The Caveman
Ordeal
When It Grows Dark

WHEN IT GROWS DARK

Jorn Lier Horst

Translated by

Anne Bruce

SANDSTONEPRESS
HIGHLAND | SCOTLAND

First published in Great Britain in 2017
Sandstone Press Ltd
Dochcarty Road
Dingwall
Ross-shire
IV15 9UG
Scotland

www.sandstonepress.com

This translation has been published with the financial support of NORLA.

The publisher acknowledges subsidy from Creative Scotland towards
publication of this volume.

ISBN: 978-1-910985-48-9
ISBNe: 978-1-910985-49-6

Cover by Freight Design, Glasgow
Typeset by Iolaire Typography Ltd, Newtonmore
Printed and bound by CPI Group (UK) Ltd, Croydon, CR0 4YY.

WILLIAM WISTING

William Wisting is a career policeman who has risen through the ranks to become Chief Inspector in the Criminal Investigation Department of Larvik Police, just like his creator, author Jorn Lier Horst. *When It Grows Dark* is the sixth title in the series to be published in English. The first, *Dregs*, found him around fifty years old, the widowed father of grown up twins, Thomas and Line.

Thomas serves in the military while daughter Line is an investigative journalist based in Oslo. Line's career frequently intersects with her that of her father and is one of the defining features of the series. Wisting, at first apprehensive, has come to value how she can operate in ways that he cannot, often turning up unexpected clues and insights.

The setting for the series is Vestfold county on the south-west coast of Norway, an area popular with holidaymakers, where rolling landscapes and attractive beaches make an unlikely setting for crime. The principal town of Larvik, where Wisting is based, is located 105 km (65 miles) southwest of Oslo. The wider Larvik district has 41,000 inhabitants, 23,000 of whom live in the town itself, and covers 530 square km. Larvik is noted for its natural springs, but its modern economy relies heavily on agriculture, commerce and services, light industry and transportation, as well as tourism. There is a ferry service from Larvik to Hirsthals in Denmark.

By the time of *When It Grows Dark* Chief Inspector William Wisting is a seasoned and highly respected police officer with over thirty years of service behind him and retirement in sight. At the story's beginning he is found giving an introductory talk to trainee police officers, but a letter arrives and soon he is drawn into an old case, one that took place in 1983 with reverberations from even farther back in time.

Fans of William Wisting will enjoy seeing him as a recently qualified police officer, still working in the uniformed branch but keen to move into CID. He is married to Ingrid and they have baby twins, Thomas and Line, the very Line, journalist and photographer, who will go on to play such an important role in her adult life. *When It Grows Dark* therefore serves as a prequel as well as a milestone in William Wisting's career, a taster for readers new to the series as well as a welcome addition for established followers of the series.

Times shall come
Times shall pass
Generation shall follow generation

From *Beautiful Is The Earth*,
hymn by B.S. Ingemann, 1850

'Grandma died twelve years ago,' explained the woman on the other side of his desk. 'She was ninety-seven. My brother inherited the house from her. It's lain empty ever since, but this summer we began to clear things out.'

Wisting glanced at the clock. Shortly, he would take part in an assembly welcoming the new intake of student police officers to their work experience year, but when he heard the name of the woman enquiring after him in the foyer downstairs, he had asked to have her sent up.

'We found a letter addressed to you,' she continued, taking an envelope from her handbag. She laid it on the table and pushed it towards him. *Wisting* was written on it in big, round letters, in a slightly shaky hand.

'It must be for you, don't you think?'

Wisting drew the letter towards him and found that the envelope was yellowed and dry. His thoughts slipped back more than thirty years. 'Yes, it's probably for me,' he agreed.

'She had hidden it behind a framed photograph of our grandfather,' the woman said. 'That lends it some sort of significance.'

Wisting weighed the still-unopened envelope in his hand. 'You haven't read it?'

'It's not addressed to me,' she said with a smile. 'Not everyone in my family is dishonest.'

'Thanks,' he said, returning her smile.

The woman stood up, her mission accomplished, and Wisting escorted her to the door with the letter still in his hand. As soon as he was alone, he sat down and opened the envelope.

It contained two sheets of paper, each with different

handwriting. As he read both, he felt something move somewhere at the back of his mind. Refolding the papers, he tucked them into the envelope again before heading off to meet the waiting students.

The conference room was hot and clammy. Someone had opened a window but the air outside seemed even clammier.

The Chief Superintendent invited Wisting to step onto the podium. Only when he was standing there did it dawn on him that he still had the envelope in his hand.

He let his gaze run over the eager faces as he reeled off the same introductory talk he had given for the past fifteen years.

Ten of them stood in freshly ironed uniform shirts: six men and four women, one of them the grandchild of the man who had stood in Wisting's shoes when he himself had entered the police force: Maren Dokken. With no idea which of the four women she might be, he searched for a family resemblance, but found none. All the same, he suspected that it must be the blonde girl with the ponytail and full lips who was sitting in one of the chairs nearest to him. Each of the students would spend a few weeks in the Criminal Investigation Department to get a thorough grounding in the realities of practical investigative work.

When he had rounded off his customary speech, he tapped the envelope lightly on the palm of his hand. The Chief Superintendent looked across, waiting for him to step down from the podium.

'I would like to . . .' Wisting said instead, 'I would like to invite you all to help me clear up an old crime mystery, one that will soon be a hundred years old.'

33 YEARS EARLIER

1

The bank card was ejected from the ATM, and *Temporarily out of order* appeared in big white letters on the screen. Wisting turned to Ingrid, who was rocking the twins in their pram. 'It must have run out of money,' he said, as he scanned the Christmas crowds thronging the street.

With a smile, Ingrid tossed her head back and peered up at the dark evening sky. Almost imperceptibly, it had started to snow. Tiny, papery flakes seemed almost poised in the air. 'We can have waffles when we get home,' she said.

Wisting tucked the card back inside his wallet. He did not have much money left in his account, and it crossed his mind that he would have to take on a few extra overtime shifts.

Putting his arm around Ingrid, he used the other to steer the pram. The twins would soon be six months old. Thomas was fast asleep, while Line was still wide-awake. She lay there, eyes blinking, trying to take in everything going on in the world around her.

He pushed the pram forward, out into Tollbodgaten, and turned in the direction of the cobbled square below the church where the town's huge, twinkling Christmas tree stood.

The stallholders in the square wore Santa hats and an enticing aroma of mulled wine, freshly baked waffles, and porridge sprinkled with sugar and cinnamon wafted from their stalls. A group of seven or eight brass players, dressed as Christmas elves, played carols from the back seat of an open, signal-red veteran car. No one could miss them.

'There's Rupert's Packard!' Ingrid exclaimed, pointing at the old vehicle.

'He's playing the trumpet,' Wisting said, smiling, as he nodded

1

to the man in the driving seat sporting a Santa beard and hat.

They stood and listened to the music.

Rupert Hansson was a friend of Ingrid's father. He had played a trumpet solo in the church at their wedding, and chauffeured them in his vintage car after the ceremony. The car, fire-engine red with green circles round the chromium-plated hubcaps, had been decorated for the occasion with birch sprigs and white ribbons.

'It's doubtful whether the old engine will start afterwards,' Wisting remarked, rubbing his hands together.

Ingrid leaned into the pram to check that the twins were comfortable and cosy before moving to Wisting's side to stand with her head resting on his shoulder.

Spotting them, Rupert Hansson tipped his Santa hat with his free hand. As Wisting waved back, he noticed that the musician was signalling for them to wait.

When the band finished playing, Rupert turned to the others, indicating that they should pack up.

Wisting and Ingrid wheeled the pram over. Rupert stepped from the car and peered in – Line had managed to extricate one hand from the quilt and was waving with her mitten, while Thomas slept soundly by her side.

'First Christmas,' Rupert said, looking up at Ingrid. 'That'll be lovely.'

'We're looking forward to it,' she answered.

Wisting walked a few paces towards the veteran car. 'I thought it was just for use in the summer months.'

'It is,' Rupert said, with a nod, walking back to the car. 'But this is a tradition. We always play at the Christmas market.'

Picking up an instrument case from the foot well beside the pedals, he set it down on the seat to open it. 'I wanted to ask you something,' he began, placing his trumpet inside.

'What's that?' Wisting asked.

'Whether you could find out who owns the old barn out at Tveidalskrysset?'

2

Wisting pictured the place, but could not recall having seen any barn. 'Is there a barn there?'

'It'll soon be in ruins,' Rupert speculated. 'It probably won't stand up to another winter of heavy snow.'

Wisting thrust his hands into his jacket pockets: 'Why do you want to know who owns it?'

'It seems there's an old car inside,' Rupert answered. 'I'm on the lookout for a restoration project.'

'Aren't there any houses in the vicinity? Somebody you could ask?'

Rupert shook his head. 'I thought you might be able to find out for me. Surely the police have registers of that kind of thing?'

'It's the Registry Office that holds those records,' Wisting said. 'You could ask there.'

'What kind of car is it supposed to be?' Ingrid asked.

'I'm not absolutely sure,' Rupert said, 'but they say it's an old Minerva.' He realised that neither Wisting nor Ingrid had heard of the vehicle marque. 'A Belgian maker,' he explained. 'They went bankrupt before the war. King Haakon's first car was a four-cylinder 1913 model Minerva.'

'Are they rare?'

Rupert nodded. 'There were never many of them in Norway. Most likely, the King's car was eventually scrapped. In any case, nobody knows what became of it.'

'How did you learn about the car out in Tveidal?'

'Mostly rumour. One of the old guys in the club heard about it from an uncle – that it had been reversed into the barn, covered with a tarpaulin and has remained there ever since.'

'When did that happen?'

'Some time in the nineteen-twenties.'

Wisting raised his eyebrows. 'It's been there for sixty years?'

Rupert nodded enthusiastically. 'If it's true, it might well be totally original and still in good condition.'

Wisting had never been particularly interested in cars. He

3

and Ingrid drove a six-year-old Volvo. However, he grew curious about why this rare vehicle had been stowed away in a barn and subsequently kept there in secret.

'Would you take a trip out to the barn with me for a look?' Rupert asked. 'Then I can explain its exact whereabouts.'

'In that car?' Wisting indicated the old Packard.

Rupert laughed. 'No, I'll winch that one up on the trailer,' he replied, pointing at the car park where a Land Rover sat in wait with a vehicle trailer behind it.

Wisting glanced across at Ingrid and the pram. All around them, stallholders had begun to close and pack up their stalls. 'Another time,' he answered.

'Just go ahead, William!' Ingrid said, brushing a few snowflakes off the pram hood. 'I can drive home with the children.'

She probably thought the same as he did: that they owed Rupert Hansson a favour. He had refused to accept payment either for playing at their wedding or driving them to the reception.

'I'll give you a lift home afterwards,' Rupert said.

'All right, then.'

Wisting took the car keys from his trouser pocket and handed them to Ingrid. He would have to snatch a few hours of sleep before going on night shift, but a trip out to Tveidal would not take very long.

Ingrid accepted the keys and gave him a peck on the cheek. 'I'll have waffles ready when you get home,' she said cheerfully.

The pram wheels left thin tracks in the snow as she trundled away.

Rupert Hansson set off to fetch the Land Rover. Wisting guided him up to the old Packard and they winched the veteran car up onto the trailer's flat bed.

Wisting clambered into the passenger seat. 'I'll drive home and drop off the trailer first,' Rupert told him.

They drove west along Helgeroveien. The snow fell more heavily, but at the same time the weather seemed milder. The asphalt was bare and wet in the tracks left by tyres on the road.

At Nalum, Rupert turned from the main road to reverse in front of a detached garage. A woman who appeared at a window lit up by an Advent star peered out at them.

Wisting stepped from the car and pushed open the heavy garage door. Rupert reversed inside before jumping out to disconnect the trailer. Two minutes later, they were on the road again.

Rupert switched on the radio but the signal was poor and the loudspeakers made a loud, crackling noise.

'The local radio station doesn't reach as far as this,' he said, turning the channel finder until he located NRK. He modulated the volume and turned to Wisting. 'I took a run out there in the autumn. It's a long time since anyone was inside that barn. It's almost completely overgrown, and the surrounding trees have grown to quite a height.'

'Is it possible to go inside?'

'There's a massive padlock on the door,' Rupert told him. 'But there are gaps between some of the timbers on the walls.' He pointed over his shoulder with his thumb. 'I've brought a couple of flashlights. We can shine them in to see whether there's anything that looks like a car on the inside.'

The next fifteen minutes passed in silence, until Rupert turned off on to Brunlanesveien. A kilometre or so later, they reached the Tveidal intersection, where he manoeuvred the car onto an overgrown side track. The car headlights picked out slender tree trunks and, at the end of the short track in front of them, they saw a barn with a saddleback roof made of rusty, corrugated metal.

2

Rupert Hansson opened the car door to retrieve two sturdy flashlights from the rear seat. Wisting followed him out of the car and glanced towards the main road, from which the old building was just about visible. Rupert left the engine running and the lights on. The snow had not yet settled among the trees.

They followed an old tyre track up to the barn, while the car headlights threw their long shadows ahead of them.

The entire eastern wall and parts of the roof were choked with leafless climbing plants.

It was a mistake to call this a barn, Wisting thought. There was no farm in the locality, and it was more reminiscent of an enormous tool shed, perhaps built to house tractors and other forestry equipment.

Rupert pointed his flashlight beam at the broad double doors, where an iron bolt stretched across, fastened on one side with a chain and padlock.

Wisting strode over and gripped the padlock, his fingers staining brown as flakes of rust loosened and peeled off. It probably would not take more than a blow from a hammer or stone to break the lock open.

Letting it go, he followed Rupert Hansson to the west side of the building. The forest had crept all the way to the wall, and they had to force their way forward through thick undergrowth.

There were no windows on the old building but, around the middle of the western wall, some of the timbers had been separated by a fallen tree. Rupert grabbed one of the branches and hauled himself up on the broken trunk beside the wall.

Wisting remained on the ground, watching as he balanced and inched his way forward. He directed the beam of light at the hole in the wall and leaned into it.

Wisting found a gap between two timbers, too narrow for him to insert the flashlight, but he put one eye to it and followed the beam from Rupert's torch. There seemed to be only a vast space inside. The light slid past an old plough with two blades, a horse-drawn cart, a wooden stool, a zinc tub, and a wheelbarrow missing its wheel. Chains and thick ropes with pulleys and hooks hung from the roof beams. On the opposite wall, a ladder was propped up with fishing nets and a couple of pale green glass balls suspended from the rungs.

The beam of light travelled continuously around the barn, too quickly for his eye to focus. For a fraction of a second, the light flickered over the interior of the doors they had already tried and Wisting thought he could make out a chain and padlock, as if they were also locked from the inside.

The light shifted to the inner part of the barn, shining on four dirty tractor tyres stacked one on top of the other. He could also see a paraffin lamp on top of a barrel only a few metres from where he stood.

Wisting moved along the wall slightly, bending a few branches to find a broader gap between the timbers. He was using his own flashlight now, shining it on the interior barn doors. His eyes had not deceived him. A chain was threaded through two iron hoops and secured with a padlock.

He returned his focus to the paraffin lamp on the barrel, where he saw a box of matches and one or two small items, but could not make them out clearly.

'There's something behind there,' Rupert yelled.

Wisting guided his light beam to meet Rupert's. Behind several empty potato crates, he could make out the top of a dusty canvas sheet.

Rupert jumped down from the tree trunk. 'We'll try to go around,' he said.

They pushed their way through dense vegetation and around the corner to the rear of the building. Wisting put his flashlight to a chink between two planks and peered inside. It smelled of rot. He could not only see potato crates and the rigging suspended from the ceiling, but also the side of something covered over.

'It might well be an old car,' he said, letting the light hug its contours. The vehicle was elevated at the back, while the front section was considerably lower, like the bonnet of a classic vintage car.

'Train the light on the floor,' Rupert requested, staring through a smaller gap.

Wisting brought the light down. The tarpaulin hung all the way to the floor over most of its length, but at the rear it was lopsided, leaving a short distance between floor and canvas. The space was just wide enough to disclose a decidedly flat car tyre.

3

The smell of freshly cooked waffles met Wisting at the front door when he arrived home. He went to the kitchen and embraced Ingrid. 'Have you put the children to bed?'

'Thomas is sleeping,' she said. 'Line's in the playpen.'

In the living room, Line lay on her stomach on a blanket behind the bars of the playpen, among rattles and soft toys. She pulled herself up and gave her father an inquisitive look.

Ingrid followed with the plate of waffles. 'Would you like coffee with them?'

He shook his head. 'I need to catch some sleep before I go on duty,' he told her, lifting a gurgling, kicking Line out of the playpen.

'Did you discover anything?'

Wisting sat down. 'There's an old car out there all right.' He perched Line on his lap. 'Rupert was really fired up about it.'

Before settling into the armchair opposite him, Ingrid lit the first Advent candle on the candelabra in the centre of the table. 'Do you know any more about who owns the barn?'

'We could have asked at the neighbouring farm, but it looked as if the family had visitors.'

'It can't be too difficult to find out?'

'The problem is that there's no specific address, and we don't know the farm registration details or land number.' He helped himself to a waffle. 'I offered to drop into the local council offices after tonight's shift to look at their maps.'

They sat chatting until Ingrid blew out the Advent candle, took Line from his knee and left the room to change her nappy.

Wisting stepped into what would in time become a children's

room, where they kept the bed settee he used when he was on late shifts. For the present, the twins slept in separate cots in their parents' bedroom. He stretched out under the blanket, set the alarm clock, switched off the light and closed his eyes, but sleep eluded him.

He was thinking about the old car in the barn and the doors that were locked on the inside. For Rupert Hansson, the most important thing had been to discover who owned it and whether he could buy it. Wisting was more inquisitive about who had left the car there and concealed it under a tarpaulin ... and how on earth could the barn doors be locked on both the inside and the outside?

The sound of a baby's crying broke into his thoughts. The noise came from the living room but whether it was Line or Thomas he couldn't tell. He waited for silence to be restored, but the opposite happened. The noise level rose in volume and intensity. He threw aside the blanket and got to his feet.

Ingrid was in the living room, sitting in the armchair with Line suckling. Thomas, on the other hand, was lying on the blanket with legs drawn up, screaming at the top of his lungs, impatient for his turn.

Wisting lifted him and let the baby's soft head snuggle against his stubbly chin. The crying turned into gurgling noises and Thomas smiled. Both babies smiled frequently now, and these smiles were not simply grimaces. They were growing fast, acquiring their own personalities, and broke into smiles at anyone's approach.

'Thank you,' Ingrid whispered from her chair.

Line twisted her head to see what was going on, with milk trickling from her mouth. 'She's finished,' Ingrid said. 'Can you take her?'

Setting Thomas on her lap, Wisting took charge of Line, walking to and fro, jiggling, patting and stroking her back until she burped. He carried her through to the bedroom and laid her in her cot before padding back to his own bed.

10

It felt as if the alarm clock rang just as he fell asleep. Fumbling in the dark, he switched it off and planted his feet on the cold floor. Before he headed for the bathroom to shave, he looked in on Ingrid and the children.

The bread bin in the kitchen was empty. Instead of buttering himself a slice of bread, he took out a packet of crispbread and ate a dry rusk standing by the window. He stuffed the rest of the packet into his briefcase.

Only a centimetre or two of snow lay on the ground, and the thermometer on the window ledge showed how the temperature had climbed as the night advanced.

At quarter to eleven he let himself into the police station in Prinsegata, where he made for the locker room to change into his uniform, glancing in the mirror to adjust his tie before continuing to the duty room.

The Duty Sergeant had already arrived and taken over from the outgoing sergeant. Erling Storvolden was a heavyset man with a round face, now approaching retirement.

'Has anything happened?' Wisting asked.

'Two road accidents,' the other officer said, picking up his cap on his way to the door. 'The roads are like glass.'

Wisting walked over to the kitchenette. As the youngest officer, it fell to him to make the coffee.

Per Haugen turned up when it was ready. Twelve years older than Wisting, he had three stripes on his epaulettes. Apart from that, his uniform shirt was crumpled and splashed with stains.

Erling Storvolden asked them to join him in perusing the logbook. There was no one else present: just two on patrol and one duty sergeant.

Storvolden lit a cigarette and declared at once that no special reports had been filed.

The past twenty-four hours had kicked off with a scuffle in a restaurant that had sent a forty-four-year-old man into custody on a drunk and disorderly charge. A drunk driver had been stopped in Kongegata, and the patrol had been called out

11

after a report of domestic violence at a house in Torstrand. Late at night, a group of teenagers had been caught in a basement where they were in the process of breaking into a storeroom. They were driven to the police station and picked up by their parents. On Sunday morning, a report had been received about a lost dog. Apart from this list the day had been quiet. Immediately after twelve, a report had been submitted about a theft from a construction site north of the town.

'A digger was stolen,' Storvolden read aloud from the logbook.

'A digger?' Haugen repeated, raising his eyebrows.

Storvolden squinted at the papers through a cloud of cigarette smoke. 'A Volvo BM 1240. You know? One of those digging machines with a snowplough on the front,' he confirmed. 'Left parked with the keys in the ignition.'

'Who the hell steals one of them?' Haugen wondered. 'It must be a drunken prank.'

They continued through the lists. The police log book was, in a sense, a distorting mirror held up to everyday life in town: theft, vandalism, fraud, assault, drunk driving, road accidents, threatening behaviour, housebreaking, driving off the road, false alarms involving emergency flares, abuse, dealing with homelessness, mentally ill people, car crashes, and obvious intoxication. It provided a multi-faceted picture of the shady side of life. Police work was marked by encounters with everything negative: the sick, the destructive, and the deviant. In many ways, Wisting revelled in the darkness. He liked to be the person on the spot when needed, to have importance for other people and at the same time safeguard society. It felt meaningful.

Storvolden rounded off the discussion by handing the patrol car keys to Haugen.

'Keep an eye out for that Volvo digger,' he said, with a smile. He stubbed out his cigarette in the ashtray, swivelled his chair towards his desk and inserted a blank sheet into the typewriter.

Before they drove into the night, the two officers spent an

hour or so on the settee in the staffroom. The police station was equipped with an aerial that picked up two channels from their neighbouring country, Sweden, where broadcasts ended later than NRK's, the Norwegian national broadcaster. On Sunday evenings, there was usually a film.

Wisting did not enjoy spending his working hours in front of a TV screen but, as the youngest member of the team, he was in no position to change such an ingrained habit and chase the older officers from the settee and into the streets.

He preferred to use his time reading records of solved cases in the archives. This educated him in the local criminal environment as well as providing insight into investigative work. He longed to be up on the first floor, in the Criminal Investigation Department but, while Ingrid was still at home with the twins, he would have to delay any application. A job as an investigator would automatically add two extra increments to his salary, but the loss of evening, night and weekend allowances would mean that he would be less well paid, and access to overtime would be cut.

It was almost one o'clock when Haugen rose from the settee and announced it was time to go for a drive. Wisting packed his belongings into his locker before pulling on his jacket and following his colleague down to the garage.

Haugen turned down Prinsegata, into Thaulowsvingen and out into Storgata. The evening train from Oslo had just unloaded a handful of passengers. Haugen let the vehicle glide slowly past and Wisting studied their faces, recognising several. There was nothing of concern. Haugen drove on through the deserted streets.

This aimless patrolling of the streets in a police car made Wisting uneasy. There was nothing especially deterrent about it, nor did it have much to do with investigation. They simply drove around waiting for something to happen. Of course, some form of guard duty and preparedness for emergency was essential, but he felt that it could be conducted in a more

13

effective fashion. It could be more focused. As he had learned from his reading, crime in Larvik seemed to be concentrated in specific areas and committed by specific culprits, usually at specific times of day. Patterns existed that should be easy to pin down and could enable them to beat the criminals to the punch.

'Could we drive along Hoffs gate?' he asked.

Haugen was watching a stray dog wandering along the kerb. 'Anything happening there?' he asked when they had driven past.

'I don't know,' Wisting answered. 'A lot of cars have been stolen from this area. The reports usually come in on Monday mornings. A couple of days go by, and then they're found trashed. They've mostly been vehicles belonging to the night shift at the Larvik Pigment factory.'

Per Haugen glanced at him, at first slightly taken aback, before grinning broadly. 'Then we'll catch them red-handed,' he said, and took the first left turn.

Six minutes later they pulled into Hoffs gat, with Larvik Commercial School and Fram Stadium on the right-hand side. On the left was a row of semi-detached houses that belonged to the local housing association. Advent stars twinkled in every other window, and some had brightly decorated Christmas trees in their gardens.

Farther along were huge concrete apartment blocks. A boy in his early twenties, already convicted of both burglary and car theft, lived in one of them. Wisting had submitted a memo about it to the Criminal Investigation Department, but did not know if they had taken any action.

A solitary lamppost cast a pale light over the car park in front of the chemicals factory. They rolled slowly past the cars belonging to the late shift.

'It seems quiet,' Haugen commented.

Wisting glimpsed the clock on the dashboard. Almost half past two. 'Maybe we're too early,' he said, looking at the Norwegian State Railways employees' houses on the opposite

14

side of the street. 'We could reverse in there and wait with the engine off.'

Haugen did not reply, but manoeuvred the patrol car into a secluded spot. He switched off the ignition, but the green light on the radio display remained on. Wisting covered it with a newspaper to ensure they were in total darkness.

Noises from the melting shop within the factory perimeter reached them from time to time. A delivery van drove past, and soon afterwards a taxi followed the same route.

After twenty minutes, it grew chilly inside the car. Wisting rubbed his hands together. Eventually this felt just as hopeless, sitting idly in a parked car, as had driving around at random.

'How long should we give them?' Haugen asked, smothering a yawn.

Wisting shrugged. 'A bit longer,' he answered, letting his eyes roam along Hoffs gate.

The streetlights shed a dull glimmer on the wet asphalt. Parked cars, trees and rubbish bins cast irregular shadows, but something seemed to be moving beside a group of mailboxes on a wooden frame.

Wisting sat upright, knowing that it might have been a gust of wind that stirred the evergreen bushes into life. 'There!' he said, now certain.

Haugen peered in the same direction. A dark, skulking figure emerged from somewhere around the high-rise blocks and crossed the road, darting glances over his shoulder and skirting along the fence towards the chemicals factory.

The distance from the police car to the car park was a bit less than one hundred metres. If he tried to steal one of the cars he would have a start on them, as they would have to turn on the engine and rev up. In addition, he had several routes to choose from if he ran, places impossible for them to follow in the car.

'I'm going out,' Wisting said.

Haugen nodded as he placed his hands on the steering wheel.

15

Wisting flicked the interior light switch to off before opening the door a tiny crack.

As he stepped out of the car, the police radio crackled into life. '6-0-3, this is 2-0,' Duty Sergeant Storvolden called out.

Haugen tweaked the volume knob but too late: the sound carried extremely well through the night. The man stopped and looked in their direction.

'Drive to Stavern!' Storvolden ordered without waiting for a response. 'I'll be back with more information.'

Haugen started the car, catching the potential car thief in the headlights. Wisting resumed his seat and unhooked the microphone. The announcement suggested urgency, probably some break-in or violent crime in progress and Storvolden would be receiving details as he called.

'Over,' he said into the microphone.

The patrol car accelerated forward. The man on the opposite side of the street shrank towards the fence, glancing from one side to the other, as if considering which way to run but, in the end, standing still. Wisting glimpsed his pallid face, enough to be able to recognise him another time. Fastening his seatbelt, he turned on the blue lights.

4

Haugen revved up the Corsa and put the pedal to the floor, but skidded at the first intersection. Road conditions were slippier than he had thought. The vehicle swerved sideways, threatening to spin all the way round. He turned the steering wheel and controlled the skid.

This did not slow their response to the emergency call-out. Their tyres squelched furiously on the road surface, and streams of water sprayed behind them. They passed Storgata and took a left turn at the railway tunnel onto Stavernveien.

The police radio crackled: '6-0-3, this is 2-0.'

Wisting sat with the microphone on his knee. 'Reading you.'

'It's a Volvo digger,' Storvolden said, 'They've driven it into the wall at the Sparebank premises. The caller is watching from the first floor of a neighbouring building. The driver is wearing a mask. Another man is standing by, waiting for the hole to get big enough.'

Wisting felt an adrenaline surge as his mouth went dry. 'Armed?'

'Negative.'

'We're at Tenvik,' Wisting said, glancing at the speedometer. 'We'll be there in four minutes.'

'Three,' Haugen corrected, stepping on the gas.

'I've got the caller on the line,' Storvolden explained. 'They're still in action.'

Blue lights flashed rhythmically in the darkness on either side of the patrol car and Haugen's knuckles were white on the steering wheel. Wisting gritted his teeth. He had no idea what awaited them or how they would tackle it. In an encounter with a Volvo digger used as a ramming tool, they would have little to contribute.

The patrol car shook at this pace, almost turning over as it crested the last hill before Stavern town centre.

Storvolden was still on the radio: 'They've taken the night safe. It seems there are two men. They've loaded the contents into a black Ford Sierra, and they're about to drive away.'

Racing round the final corner they found half of the street in front of them was strewn with bricks and rubble. A yellow digger with huge rear wheels was parked on the pavement with its bucket lowered, a massive hole gaping in the wall of the bank where the night safe deposit slot had been. An alarm was wailing.

One of the robbers slammed the boot shut and leapt into the Sierra as it took off.

'We're on the spot,' Wisting declared, noting the exact time. He read out the getaway car's registration number, watching it swerve sideways out of the street, accelerating rapidly.

Wisting's head banged on the ceiling as Haugen drove over the bricks.

The black Sierra, in better condition than the old patrol car, rapidly increased its lead. However, what the police vehicle lacked in power, it made up for in manoeuvrability. They gained an advantage with every corner, but on flat stretches the getaway car pulled away.

Wisting continually reported their position to Storvolden, aware that they were alone in their pursuit. Once the car crossed into a different police authority, they could reckon on a roadblock being set up or a spike mat rolled out.

Approaching the sharp bends before Askeskogen, Haugen shifted down a gear and moved the car to the edge of the road in the hope of reducing the robbers' lead. Suddenly the left wheels slipped beyond the asphalt, and Wisting steeled himself for the vehicle leaving the road, which he thought was imminent. Miraculously, Haugen managed to return the car to the road, but lost control of both steering wheel and direction in the process. It lurched sideways before doing a 180-degree turn and coming to a shuddering stop.

Haugen swore loudly as he turned in reverse gear, veering from side to side before the tyres gripped. When they emerged on to a straight stretch, the black Sierra was gone.

'We've lost them,' Wisting reported. Storvolden did not respond. Most likely he was busy on the telephone, sounding the alarm in neighbouring districts.

Haugen maintained a steady speed, but the wooded area they were now driving through was intersected with minor byways and off-road tracks. Escape was easy.

When they came out at the Helgeroa crossroads, Haugen brought the car to a halt, swearing again as he hammered both fists on the steering wheel. The stench of burning clutch filled the compartment.

Wisting switched off the blue lights. A pair of car headlights appeared on the road leading from Nevlunghavn. They sat watching as they approached.

'They've probably swapped cars,' Wisting said, without taking his eyes off the headlights.

'Think so?'

Wisting responded with a nod. He was reluctant to be a know-all but, in every successful robbery he had read about, a change of getaway vehicle was part of the plan.

The car coming towards them took the recognisable shape of a Volkswagen Beetle. 'Do you think that's them?' Haugen said, grinning.

As the car passed, their headlights illuminated the interior. The elderly woman in the driver's seat turned her head and stared at them, wide-eyed, keeping both hands on the wheel.

Haugen put the car in gear and began a turn as a prelude to driving back to the crime scene.

'Wait!' Wisting said, pointing north, where the sky had taken on an orange glow.

Haugen twisted the steering wheel to jolt the car into the required direction. Wisting switched on the blue lights again and shortly afterwards they overtook the grey Volkswagen.

The blaze was about a kilometre ahead and, as they drove, the orange glow increased in intensity.

Wisting had driven that same stretch of road the previous evening, *en route* to the barn that contained the veteran car.

As they approached the crossroads at Tveidal, his suppositions were proved correct. Halfway along the track to the barn, a car was on fire.

Haugen stopped on the asphalt road, thirty metres away, and Wisting jumped out into the eye-stinging smoke of burning rubber. He quickly rounded the police car to take the fire extinguisher from the boot. Elongated, pale-blue flames darted through the shattered windows of the black Sierra. Fierce heat made it impossible to approach the blaze.

From within the patrol car, Wisting could hear Haugen telling Storvolden that the robbers had set the getaway car on fire, and requesting him to call the fire brigade.

Wisting shielded his eyes. The light from the explosive inferno was intense. Waves of thick, black smoke billowed into the dark night.

Flames spread to the surrounding vegetation, and a crooked pine tree caught alight. The distance from the car to the barn was identical to that from the fire to the spot where Wisting was standing. There was a risk that it might spread in that direction.

Haugen stepped from the patrol car, covering his nose and mouth with his hand. Behind them, the Volkswagen had drawn to a halt at the road verge.

They watched the fire from a distance, the wind gusting towards the barn, the flames creeping steadily closer.

When the woman in the Volkswagen came out, Wisting went to speak to her. 'Do you know who owns the barn?'

At that moment, something inside the Sierra's engine exploded and a wave of hot air blew towards them. They moved even further away, and Wisting repeated his question.

'Knut Heian,' she answered. 'He lives just down the road. Do you want me to drive there and let him know?'

Wisting nodded and she clambered into her car again, pulled on her safety belt and drove off.

The intensity of the fire subsided as quickly as it had grown, but the barn was out of danger. When the first fire tender appeared ten minutes later, the flames were dying out by themselves.

The fire crew flung out hoses, connected them and attacked what was still burning, water from the hoses making the remaining flames flare up before folding into themselves like flowers.

A couple of cars with inquisitive spectators had parked at the road verge, but they drove off when the drama petered out. A little flatbed truck came driving towards the intersection, followed by the ancient Volkswagen Beetle. Both vehicles stopped behind the fire tender and a man in his fifties leapt down from the truck. His hair was all over the place; his sleep had been disturbed.

Wisting crossed over to meet him. 'Are you the landowner?'

The man confirmed that this was the case, peering over Wisting's shoulder at the fire.

'It's taken some of the scrub,' Wisting told him, 'but the barn is unscathed.'

The man ran his hand through his hair. 'What actually happened?'

The woman from the Volkswagen stood within hearing distance.

'The car was used in a break-in at the Sparebank branch in Stavern,' Wisting said. 'They probably had another car here, and they've changed vehicles.'

The man took a few steps beyond Wisting for a better look. 'Have you noticed anything unusual around here in the past few days?' Wisting asked. 'Parked cars or anything like that?'

'I don't use the hay barn,' the man explained, not really answering the question.

Wisting turned to face the woman from the Volkswagen and repeated his question. If she drove past here often she might have noticed something. She pondered this but nothing came to mind.

Wisting produced his notebook and jotted down their names, addresses and phone numbers.

Haugen, who had been standing with the fire crew, now waved Wisting over.

'The fire brigade will cordon this off,' he said. 'Storvolden has called out personnel from CID. We have to go back to the bank and secure the crime scene until the technicians arrive.'

A photographer from the local newspaper turned up before they drove away. The smell from the fire was starting to give Wisting a headache, and he knew that his hair and uniform would stink for days to come.

'There are two roads they could have taken,' Haugen suggested. 'West, through Tveidalen and across to Telemark, or north and on to the E18.'

Wisting agreed, but there was a third alternative: that the robbers had taken refuge in a house nearby. There was always risk when you were on the move. The chances of being caught were great, especially at night with a minimum of traffic on the roads. If the police emergency plan was followed to the letter, blocks would be set up on all roads leading from the area. The robbery had been professionally executed. Everything indicated that they knew what they were doing.

It started snowing as they returned to Stavern. Tiny snowflakes whirled through the air. Three bank employees were pacing about in the street, gathering the papers and documents that had been scattered over the road. Wisting recognised Leon Prytz, the bank manager, who approached them as they parked. Haugen remained behind the wheel, giving Storvolden information via the police radio, while Wisting stepped out.

All that was left of the night safe itself was twisted metal.

'We're pretty well protected against robbery and break-in,' the bank manager told him. 'But not against this.'

'How much money might be involved?'

The bank manager shrugged. 'There's a lot of cash in circulation at present,' he said. 'People are doing Christmas shopping. Lots of shop owners put the whole week's takings into the night safe for the weekend. We'll need every single customer to report before we can calculate an exact sum.'

'But a rough estimate?'

The bank manager hesitated before answering: 'I'd think there would be about two million kroner, probably a bit more than that.'

Wisting took a deep breath. He earned just less than one hundred and twenty thousand in annual salary. Two million was a great deal of fast money for the thieves.

'How does the night safe actually function?' he asked.

'In principle, the same way as a post box. Businesses that have an arrangement with us put their takings into a sealed bag and drop it into the slot in the wall. There's a locked gate arrangement that prevents the bags being fished out again, and they remain lying inside a metal compartment.'

'Is it locked?'

'Yes, of course. A locked compartment in a locked room, but it's not a safe or a strongroom. Once they had breached the wall, it was a relatively simple matter to open the storage compartment.'

Wisting took notes. Neither the bank nor the police had been prepared, but they should have been aware of the possibility that this might happen. There had been similar robberies in other locations in the Østland region – in Akershus, Asker, Bærum, Buskerud and Romerike, a geographical spread around the capital city. It suggested an organised gang based in Oslo, or possibly other criminals who had copied their method. They should have seen this coming as surely as a meteorologist could forecast bad weather.

23

5

Wisting began writing his report around half past six, having already given a verbal account to the detective squad.

Using two fingers he pecked his way across the keyboard. Tired as he was, the words came sluggishly, even though he followed a standard template: time and place of notification, the call-out, what he had seen, who he had spoken to, and what they had told him. If he had initiated the investigation he would have begun with the black Sierra. It had probably been stolen, which would be a starting point. The same applied to the Volvo digger. Someone might have seen something on the construction site where it had been stolen, or the culprits might have left traces. The second getaway car had most likely also been stolen, and they could make a list of all possible vehicles. Finally, he listed the unsolved cases that used the same *modus operandi* in other police districts.

After half an hour's overtime, he tugged the sheet of paper out of the typewriter and left it in the CID pigeonhole.

It was still dark when he went home. At this time of year, night shift meant living in constant darkness. The sun did not come up until you had gone to bed in the early morning, and it set before you woke again in the afternoon.

He arrived home to be met by a baby crying. Thomas was lying in the playpen while Line was being fed. He took him on his knee, but that did not stop his sobbing.

'He probably won't stop until he's been fed,' Ingrid said.

Although unflappable, she was also exhausted. He knew she would not have had much sleep.

24

'I found out who owns that old barn,' he said, and described the night's events.

Thomas quietened down after a while, and Wisting took him to Ingrid when she was ready. They exchanged babies, and Wisting laid Line across his shoulder before pacing the living room.

'Have you told Rupert?' Ingrid asked.

Wisting shook his head. 'I'll phone him this afternoon.'

Line gave a loud burp, and warm milk spread across his shoulder.

Ingrid smiled. 'She has to have a bath anyway.'

Heading for the bathroom, he laid his daughter on the changing table and watched her while he took off his shirt and filled the bathtub with lukewarm water. He stripped off her clothes, lifted her into the tub and lowered her carefully in. Delighted, she gave a scream of pleasure, kicking her chubby legs and gasping when water splashed on her face.

'When are you going back to work?' Ingrid called through.

'In two or three days,' he answered. It was a depressing thought. The investigation would be at it most hectic in the first few days and he would prefer to be involved, but his job was over and done when the report was written.

He took Line out of the water and cradled her small, naked body against his chest, before using his spare hand to locate a towel and wrap it around her. Soon she was stretched out on her back in the playpen – dry, in clean pyjamas, hunger satisfied. After a struggle, she turned onto her front and examined her toys.

'I'll do Thomas,' Ingrid said, standing up. 'You go to bed.'

He went to the bed settee in the spare room and lay down, feeling that he had forgotten to include something in his report. Something significant. It niggled him so much that he took a while to fall asleep. When he woke six hours later, the thought lingered.

As he pulled on a T-shirt, he felt some tenderness on his chest from the chafing of his seat belt during the car chase.

25

It must have been snowing the entire time he was asleep and, outside the kitchen window, plump snowflakes were still falling from the sky.

Ingrid went out to the mailbox. The newspaper boy pushed his bike through the snow. Normally the newspaper was delivered before three o'clock. Now it was after half past.

He looked through the post, already spread across the kitchen worktop, but saw nothing of interest.

Ingrid stamped the snow off her feet and came inside.

'They were talking about it on the radio news,' she said, putting the newspaper down on the kitchen table. The front page was facing up and showing a picture of the bank with the Volvo digger in front of the demolished wall.

Wisting drew the paper towards him and leafed through to more photos of the bank and the blazing car at Tveidalskrysset. They must have been taken before snow blanketed the ground.

He skimmed the text, but understood that the journalists had not discovered anything new about the case.

Ingrid put on a pan of potatoes.

'Are the children sleeping?' he asked.

'Finally,' she replied. 'They've been a bit tiresome today.'

'Well, you can go for a nap after dinner.'

He read through the rest of the newspaper: photographs and interviews of children attending the switch-on of the Christmas lights, results and reports of the day's sporting fixtures, and a considerable amount of space given to the Polish union leader Lech Wałęsa who did not dare travel to Norway to accept the Nobel Peace Prize. A lesser amount of column space contained reports about the man who had ended up arrested for being drunk and disorderly after an argument in the town centre, about the drunk driver, the house break-in, the teenagers caught red-handed in a basement storeroom and about the dog who was still missing. The final report stated that the police had received a complaint on Monday morning about a Ford Escort stolen from its parking spot outside the chemicals factory.

26

Wisting heaved a sigh, and Ingrid gave him a quizzical look. He told her that he and Haugen had been in their car, observing the person who was probably the car thief, when the alarm came in from Stavern.

'We could have caught him,' he said, shaking his head.

At that moment, a thought struck him. One of the cars stolen earlier had been a fairly new Ford Sierra, the same type as the one used by the bank robbers. He got to his feet and left the living room.

'Where are you going?' Ingrid asked.

'I just need to make a phone call,' he said, from the telephone bench.

He dialled the direct number for the Criminal Investigation Department, checking the time while he waited for someone to answer. It was outside normal working hours, but he doubted whether the Chief Inspector had gone home.

At last the phone was picked up, and Wisting recognised Ove Dokken's voice, answering in his usual abrupt and dismissive manner.

Wisting explained who he was. 'I thought of something,' he said. 'A black Ford Sierra was stolen from Hoffs gate a fortnight ago. That could be the one used last night.'

'We've got everything under control, Wisting,' Dokken replied, sounding anxious to bring the conversation to a close.

'Was it the same car?'

'Yes. It had stolen plates, but Haber located a chassis number and checked it out.'

'A lot of cars have been stolen in that vicinity,' Wisting said. 'I wrote a memo about it a week ago.'

'We're looking into it.'

'Any other news?' Wisting ventured. 'Do you have any suspects?'

'We don't have anything specific, but we're concentrating on a criminal gang in Groruddalen, east of Oslo.'

Wisting weighed up whether to mention that he had a couple

27

of days off, and that he was available if required, but the Chief Inspector beat him to it.

'This is a serious business,' he said. 'The investigation is being organised in conjunction with other police districts where they've had similar ram-raids. The Public Prosecutor has ordered a coordinated investigation, and a Kripos team from National HQ are on their way to assist. They're sending down their best officers.'

Wisting shifted the receiver to his other ear. They had used the time he had been sleeping on organisation and administration only. The actual investigation was not yet off the ground.

'Thanks for phoning,' Dokken said.

Wisting understood they had no use for him, but all the same asked Dokken to let him know if there was anything he could do. The call ended.

Ingrid was leaning on the doorframe. 'Have you called Rupert?' she asked.

The veteran car had slipped Wisting's mind. He rose from the telephone bench. 'I can do that after five o'clock.'

After dinner he took out the telephone directory and looked up Rupert's number. He explained about the coincidence of the bank robbers' vehicle being set on fire just beside the barn they had visited.

'It's not such a strange coincidence,' Rupert said, 'when it's such an ideal hiding place.'

Wisting agreed. 'All the same, the coincidence led to the owner of the barn turning up last night.'

'Did you ask him about the car?'

'No, but I have his phone number.' Wisting reached for the notebook he had left on the sideboard. 'I thought you would want to talk to him yourself,' he added, reading out the name and number.

Rupert Hansson hesitated. 'Should I phone him now, or do you think I should wait until all this business of the robbery and the fire has faded into the background?'

'I can't see any reason to wait. Phone and let me know how you get on.'

Twenty minutes later, Rupert Hansson phoned back. 'Are you doing anything tomorrow?'

'I'm off duty,' Wisting replied.

'Could you come with me to the barn? The farmer has promised to meet me there at twelve o'clock.'

Wisting needed no time to think about it. His curiosity was aroused.

6

Rupert Hansson and the landowner had already arrived when Wisting turned off the main road. Knut Heian was wearing overalls – the same ones as on the night of the fire when Wisting had spoken to him. He had used a tractor to clear the track that ran between the trees. The burned-out wreck had been towed away, and snow had blanketed most of the area, leaving only a few scorched, black tree stumps as evidence of the fire.

Stepping from his car, Wisting said hello and followed in their footsteps to the barn doors. Rupert was carrying two flashlights, and Heian had brought an axe.

'I couldn't find a key,' he said. 'I haven't been in here for at least fifteen years.'

He lifted the padlock in the same way that Wisting had done. Letting it go, he delivered a heavy blow with the back of the axe. The lock sprang open. He unhooked it, laid down the axe and pulled open the massive iron bolt. He tried to open the double doors, but something held them shut on the inside.

Wisting kept silent about having looked through cracks in the timber wall the first time he had been here, and what he had seen.

'That's odd,' Heian said.

Rupert Hansson assisted him in pulling the double doors as far out as they could manage. 'There's a chain hanging in there,' Rupert said, pointing through the gap.

Knut Heian nodded in agreement. 'Hold on to this,' he said. Entrusting the door to Wisting he grabbed the axe again, raised it above his head and aimed a well-directed swipe with the sharp edge through the narrow gap. The chain glinted and rattled, to no avail. He lifted the axe and struck again, but not until he struck a third time did something give. The chain fell to the floor on the inside, and the dry hinges creaked as the doors slid slightly ajar.

Knut Heian inspected the damage to his axe blade before taking hold of one door and yanking it open. The snow piled up behind the door impeded its movement. Rupert put his back into helping and soon both doors were wide open.

Pearly winter light spilled into the huge space as Heian kicked aside the chain on the earth floor.

Rupert Hansson switched on one of the flashlights and handed Heian the other.

The barn contained more clutter and junk than Wisting and Rupert had seen from outside. It was crammed full of boxes, packing cases and barrels, items stacked and stowed away, hidden and forgotten.

Wisting crossed to the barrel with the paraffin lamp on top. In addition to the box of matches, there was also a ballpoint pen and a postcard of sun, sea and rocky shoreline. Nothing was written on it.

Farther inside the barn, there was a cart laden with hay poles, and behind that a pile of folding chairs, a bathtub and a broken dresser. Shelves on the wall were full of paint cans, jars, rags and rusty tools.

'We played in here as kids,' Heian explained. 'There wasn't so much stuff then. It was mainly used for drying hay.' He pointed at the beams underneath the roof. 'We used to balance on those, and fought until one of us lost and fell down.' He squeezed between two potato crates. 'We made these into mazes or piled them up to build a house several storeys high.'

'When was that?' Wisting asked.

Knut Heian ran his hand through his hair. 'It must have been at the beginning of the thirties.'

'Was the car here at that time?' Rupert Hansson asked, aiming his torch into the dark recesses.

Heian nodded. 'It's been here for as long as I can remember. We often sneaked under the tarpaulin and sat behind the steering wheel. I couldn't reach the pedals, even when I perched at the front of the seat. I think I must have been five or six, so it must have been in the thirties. Long before the war.'

'And the car has been here ever since?' Rupert Hansson asked.

'I don't know any differently. It was my uncle who owned the place, and he worked mostly with timber. My father took over his farm in 1954. That's why it stayed like this. We have all the hay barns we need on our own land, so this one has never been used.'

A sheet of corrugated metal, propped on its edge, blocked their way. Heian moved the sheet aside, revealing a thin mattress, dirty and stained, with a faded, folded blanket at the foot, on the floor.

'Has anyone being sleeping here?' Wisting asked.

Heian kicked the mattress with the toe of his shoe, and a cloud of dust whirled up in the light from his torch.

'If so, it must have been a long time ago,' he answered.

Wisting glanced at the door opening and the chain lying on the floor. He reached forward and picked up the blanket. There was a newspaper and a stash of weekly magazines lying underneath. He dropped the blanket without taking a closer look at any of them, and followed the others. Heian shifted some glassless window frames to reach the vintage car. The canvas covering was dusty and spattered with bird droppings. Heian gave Wisting the flashlight and used both hands to grip the tarpaulin, tugging it towards him before lifting it to one side.

All three stood rooted to the spot until the dust had subsided.

The tarpaulin covered a classic veteran car with sleek lines, closed cabin, long bonnet and broad running board. In dilapidated condition, it was dirty and dented and far from perfect. The paintwork had once been black and glossy, but now the metal had corroded, and extensive areas were covered with a white coating that looked like salt. In some parts the metal was completely absent.

The left front wheel was rotten. The wheel brace had rusted so much that it had snapped, and the car had leaned to one side. What was left of the wheel rim was covered in green moss.

Wisting stepped forward and shone the torch inside. The grey glass was shrouded with cobwebs, and the seats looked as if they had been nibbled by mice. The stuffing was gone, and coiled springs jutted through the mottled leather upholstery.

Wisting took a step back and looked at the car from a distance. It had a dent on the left front wing, but had probably been in good, driveable condition when it had been left inside the barn.

'What make of car is it?' Knut Heian asked.

'It's a Minerva,' Rupert said. 'I've seen pictures of them. It dates from about 1915.'

'There are no plates on it,' Wisting pointed out.

Rupert made a beeline for the engine housing. 'May I?' he asked Heian, taking hold of the hinge that held the lid in place.

'Be my guest.'

The metal made a scraping noise as Rupert lifted the lid.

'How does it seem?' Wisting asked.

It looked like a simple engine: a moulded iron crankcase with fuel hose, pistons, a fan with a crumbling belt, radiator and a jumble of wires. Rupert jiggled some of the engine parts.

'Not too bad,' he said, turning to face Heian. 'Are you interested in selling?'

Knut Heian beamed. 'It's no use to me sitting in here. But I'm not so sure that it's up to me to sell it. Strictly speaking, it's not mine.'

Wisting peered into the engine cavity. 'Can you manage to locate an engine number?'

Moving the flashlight to his other hand, Rupert leaned forward again. 'Let's see ...'

Wisting turned to Heian. 'You say it's been here for as long

33

as you can remember, but do you know anything about how it got here?'

Heian ran his fingers through his hair again. 'Not really, but there was talk about the car when my father took over in 1954. Uncle Harald was still living then. Apparently, Grandpa made some arrangement to store it.'

'Do you know who this arrangement was with?'

'No, and it seemed as if the car shouldn't really be talked about. There's always been undue secrecy surrounding it. I never knew who brought it here, or why it was left, but Grandpa was probably well paid for storing it.'

'Is your grandfather still living?'

Heian laughed at the question, and it dawned on Wisting that the man would have to be more than a hundred years old.

'Okay, what was his name?'

'Peder. Peder Heian. Uncle Harald told me he once asked Grandpa about the car, but didn't get an answer. Grandpa lost his temper when he heard the question, and was so angry that Harald never mentioned it again.'

'How did you youngsters get in and out of here?'

'There's an opening in the wall - up there,' Heian answered, pointing. 'We climbed a ladder on the outside, pulled it up after us and lowered it down on the inside.'

Wisting glanced up. There was no opening now but there was a small ledge formed by a tier of beams, where there was just enough room for a few young lads to huddle together before pulling the ladder up after them.

'Now we'll see,' Rupert Hansson mumbled. He had found a rag that he used to wipe the base of the engine cavity. 'Here's the number,' he called out, reading aloud the series of numbers from the side of the engine housing.

Wisting produced his notebook. 'One more time,' he said, jotting down the numbers as Rupert rattled them off again. Some of them were difficult to read, and it took time to be sure they had them right.

'There has to be some kind of register, don't you think?' Wisting asked.

'The automobile register goes back to 1899,' Rupert informed him. 'It was established by the Oslo police force.'

'What about the number on the chassis? Where would we find that?'

'As a rule, somewhere near the driver's seat.' Rupert opened the door and, leaning in, examined the floor. A metal plate was fastened to the inside of the cabin. 'Here it is,' he said. Wisting asked him to read it out. It comprised only five digits: 55356.

Rupert Hansson sat behind the steering wheel, studying the instrument panel. Knut Heian stepped on to the running board beside him.

'What do you think it might be worth?' he asked.

Rupert hesitated, before answering: 'Difficult to say. After all, it's really a restoration project. Someone in the club embarked on a similar project a few years back. That was an old Pathfinder. I think he paid fifty thousand kroner for the car, but he spent many times that fixing it up.'

Knut Heian licked his lips. This sum amounted to half an average annual wage.

Wisting wanted to mention what Rupert had said about King Haakon driving the same make of car, but let it drop. If these two ended up discussing a sale, that little snippet might crank up the price.

He skirted round to the other side with the flashlight in his hand, and studied the dent. Obviously, the car had hit something. The front wing was pressed in, and the bodywork was scraped along the length of the whole side. The impact had probably led to a weakness in the front suspension that had later caused it to break down.

Wisting ran his hand along the collision damage to feel the depth of the scratch. Immediately above the rear wheel arch, he discovered a hole, completely circular, and slightly too small for him to poke his finger into.

Opening the rear door, he stood with his head halfway inside while he pointed the flashlight beam at the hole. The light shone through the cabin, continuing inside the car to a gash in the back of the rear seat.

He studied the entry hole again until he was sure. It was a bullet hole.

7

Parts of the tarpaulin still hung over the rear of the vehicle. Wisting tugged it off to inspect the bodywork. He was unable to find an exit hole, which told him the bullet was inside the car, somewhere behind the back seat.

Folding the tarpaulin over the rear wheel arch, he concealed the bullet hole. Back with the others he said, 'I have a suggestion. I can try to find out what happened when the car was brought in here, and who owns it. Then we can come to an arrangement of mutual benefit.'

The others were happy with this.

'In the meantime, you can leave the car here, but don't let anyone else see it,' he suggested, making eye contact with Knut Heian.

'What if you don't discover anything?' Heian asked.

'Then you're free to sell it and let Rupert take the risk that someone might turn up and claim to be the owner.'

This was an arrangement they were both willing to go along with. Wisting grabbed the tarpaulin and, with the help of the other two, drew it back over the vehicle. They left the barn together and pushed the doors closed.

'Do you have a new padlock?' Wisting asked.

'I can get one tomorrow,' Heian said, as he hooked the damaged padlock through the shackle that held the bolt in place.

Rupert Hansson held out his hand. 'Do we have a deal?'

'Deal,' Heian replied, giving them both firm handshakes.

Wisting and Rupert Hansson returned to their cars as Heian clambered into his tractor.

Wisting had held on to one of Rupert's flashlights. Backing

out from the track, he put his car in gear and accelerated rapidly, leaving the scene before Rupert began to look for it.

He drove inland towards Tveidalen, meaning to hang around for fifteen minutes or so before driving back to the barn. He wanted to examine the vintage car more closely on his own.

The road he took was one of the possible escape routes following the bank robbery, but the least likely one if Oslo criminals were involved. The road through Tveidalen ran west, towards Telemark. An Oslo gang would probably have taken the fastest route in the opposite direction.

Snow began to fall again and the wipers snicked across the windscreen. The road ahead was desolate and bare, with snow banked up on either side. He searched for a turning place. Numerous holiday cottages dotted the area, but none of the tracks had been cleared, and he considered doing a three-point turn on the main road. It did not strike him, what he had seen, until he had passed a group of mailboxes mounted on a frame.

He glanced in the mirror for confirmation – a pair of tyre tracks visible along one of the snow-covered driveways. It was a chance observation, but he had gained some experience by now and knew to trust his gut feelings.

Reducing his speed, he drove to the verge and turned, stopped at the mailboxes and stepped out. The tyre tracks led in only one direction, from the cluster of cottages to the main road. The driver had struggled to negotiate the bank of snow and had required someone's help to push the car. His conclusion was that the car must have driven in when the road was still clear, and out again after the heavy snowfall.

Wisting climbed over the bank of snow, wading out and sinking up to his knees. There were prints from a pair of large boots where a man had stood behind the car and pushed. One behind the steering wheel, and one behind the car: the two ram-raiders?

He wondered what he should do, whether he should report this to CID or follow the footprints among the trees. He chose the latter. After all, a few tracks in the snow might mean nothing at all. His observations were still too vague to justify bringing anyone else in at present.

He waded further on, following the tyre tracks. After only a few steps his boots had filled with snow. The trees on either side of the narrow track were laden and sagging towards him. After about five hundred metres, the tracks turned ninety degrees to the left and disappeared through a gate. A red-painted cottage was situated on a plateau in the steep landscape. The car had been parked between the cottage and the fence, on a rectangular space where tufts of yellow grass appeared through the sparser layer of snow. Footprints showed that whoever had been here had made several trips between the cottage and the car.

Wisting climbed onto the decking, cupped his hands on the window and peered inside. It was a simple cottage with modern pine furniture. From where he stood, he could see a coffee table, a settee and two chairs. In the centre of the room was a substantial, cast-iron wood-burning stove. He moved to the next window, where he looked in on a blue-painted kitchen with dead flies scattered on the windowsill. There were cotton runners on the worktops. Apart from that, the room contained cupboards, a kitchen table and a gas cooker. Everything was neat and tidy, as if the last occupant had been fastidious about not leaving any traces.

Wisting stood in the snow, deep in thought. The cottage was exactly what a gang of robbers would need, a place to lie low for a few hours after the raid, while they mulled things over and got some idea of the robbery proceeds. This would mean opening hundreds of night safe envelopes.

They would have to get rid of the sealed envelopes, and the pay-in slips that accompanied them, to avoid being directly connected to the bank raid.

He took another step back and looked up at the chimney. There was no snow on it, indicating that the stove had been used recently. The heat had prevented the snow from lying.

It did not necessarily mean anything. With the temperature sitting around zero, it was natural to light a fire.

A little metal plate was attached to the cottage wall, bearing a number: H292. He took out his notebook and pencil and wrote down the digits. The local authority kept a register of holiday cottages. Earlier that autumn, there had been burglaries in seventeen cottages along the Naver Fjord. Wisting had been assisted in finding the affected owners by the Building Control Department. It should be an easy matter to identify who owned cottage H292, and so learn who had been there. If he were lucky, the name and cottage number would be on one of the mailboxes by the roadside.

His thoughts drifted back to a break-in the previous year, in which the thieves had not exactly broken in, but used keys left outside. It turned out that it was a widespread practice to hide keys under a paving stone, on a shelf, under a ledge or in a wood store.

A gust of wind shook a scatter of snow from the nearest trees. Looking around, he spied an old log chair on the decking in front of the cottage. He walked across and looked underneath it, finding several dead bugs, but no key.

As he scanned the area for alternative hiding places, he noticed footprints around the cottage wall. He followed them and ran his hand along the back of the drainpipe. His hand encountered a nail with a dangling key.

Crouching down, he studied it more closely. It crossed his mind that any search would be illegal but, on the other hand, he had uncovered fresh traces. The wood stove might contain charred bank slips that were even now being slowly consumed by the dying embers.

From where he stood, he could see Mørje Fjord and Håøya Island, and in the background a gas tanker gliding along the fjord, most likely heading for one of the major industrial installations in Grenland.

It did not take him long to make up his mind. Clutching the

key, he walked purposefully to the door and inserted it in the lock. He looked over his shoulder before turning the key, and then he was inside.

The cottage was still warm, and a distinct smell of tobacco smoke hung in the air. He took a long step from the doormat to a rag rug, before removing his boots and padding onwards in his stocking feet. What he was looking for was something that might give an indication of who had been there, and whether they were linked to the robbery.

A visitors' book lay in the centre of the coffee table. Pulling the sleeve of his sweater down below his jacket to avoid leaving fingerprints, he flicked through to the last page where someone had written something, dated September 7th, and captioned *Thanks for this summer!* Whoever had been here in the last twenty-four hours had not left a message in the visitors' book.

He looked at the first few pages to see whether the owner had written anything about the place. *Welcome to Seaview*, it said. *We'd appreciate you leaving a few words after your stay. Vivian and Roger.*

That did not help much. Vivian and Roger.

The stove was no longer giving off any heat, and ash trickled out when he opened it. It was too dark to see anything inside, but he picked up a box of matches from one of the shelves, struck one and pushed it in. He saw nothing but grey ashes.

Lifting a poker, he rummaged around and lit another match, but found nothing to suggest that anything other than wood had been burned.

The cottage contained two bedrooms, one with a double bed and the other bunk beds. There was room to sleep seven altogether, but the beds were all made and the bedside tables bare.

He left the living room and entered the kitchenette where the curtains were slightly askew, as if they had been closed and not arranged properly when opened again.

A bottle of white wine was stored in the fridge. The larder was filled with cans and packets of food. The bin underneath the sink was empty.

On his return to the front door, he tripped on the rag rug. Squatting down to straighten it, he discovered a one-krone coin underneath the rug. He was about to pick it up, but on reflection decided to leave it there. Instead, he knelt, bent over and squinted under the settee. Among the balls of dust and fluff, he saw another three kroner and one larger coin.

8

Wisting remained on his knees, head tilted, staring at the coins under the settee, before standing up and gathering his thoughts.

Two men had spent some time in an out-of-the-way cottage. The curtains had been drawn. Coins had been dropped on the floor. In total, all of this fitted the hypothesis that the robbers had used this cottage as a hangout, but each element of the theory could also have many other logical explanations, and need not have anything to do with the crime. Nevertheless, it was information he could no longer keep to himself.

He left, locking the door behind him and returning the key to its previous place. He followed his own footprints back to his car and drove slowly down the narrow track to the mailboxes. They were not furnished with cottage numbers, but one of them was marked 'Vivian and Roger Brun'.

The mailbox contained a flier from a timber felling company and another from a tradesman who carried out *all kinds of maintenance*, but no addressed letters. Kripos, the national serious crime unit, had direct access to the citizens' database at Statistics Norway. Consulting them would be easier than going to the local authority headquarters to browse through their folders. In the future, he thought, it should be possible for every police district to be connected to this data system.

The old car with the bullet hole would have to wait. He drove into town and parked in the street outside the police station.

Inside the Criminal Investigation Department, it was quieter than he had anticipated, though he could hear typewriters

43

working in the nearest offices. Farther along the corridor, a burst of laughter rang out, and three men emerged from a conference room *en route* to their individual offices. They were unfamiliar to Wisting and he assumed that they were the detectives from other police districts, or from Kripos.

The Chief Inspector's office door was ajar. Ove Dokken, seated behind his desk, had a cigarette in the corner of his mouth, and was reading a report. Deep furrows lined his face, spreading in every direction, as if to mark every difficult decision he had made in his career. Wisting wished he possessed a mere fraction of the experience and knowledge that a lifetime in the police had given him.

As if sensing Wisting's presence, Dokken lifted his head and gazed at him through the fog of cigarette smoke.

Wisting stepped into the room. 'Do you have a minute?' he asked.

Dokken's eyes looked down again at the papers he was reading. 'Not really.'

'I had reason to go out to Tveidalen today,' Wisting ventured, undeterred, holding the back of the empty chair with his right hand. 'Not far from where the getaway car was set on fire.'

Dokken finished reading a sentence before setting aside the report and signalling that he was willing to hear more.

'It looked as if people had spent some time in a cottage out there, close by.'

'So?'

'Tracks in the snow had been left by a car and two people. They must have arrived before the snow fell, and had difficulty getting back to the road after the last heavy snowfall.'

The Chief Inspector appeared to be anticipating more. Wisting had decided not to tell him that he had been inside the cottage.

'Holiday cottages are mainly used only in summer,' he added. 'I thought of the bank robbers, that maybe they were the ones who had been there.'

'Great,' Dokken said, stubbing out his cigarette in an over-flowing ashtray. 'Excellent idea. Write it down and send it in to me.' He pointed at a blue document tray marked *Tip-offs*, already filled with a stack of notes.

'Okay,' Wisting agreed. 'Could I borrow an office here?'

Dokken eased another cigarette out of the packet. 'You can have Wrangsund's office,' he said, glancing over Wisting's shoulder. 'He's on sick leave and won't be back.'

The office was situated at the far end of the corridor, and looked as though it had been abandoned in haste, as if the investigator who worked there had taken ill suddenly. A note-book was open on the desk with a pen beside it. A sheet of paper remained in the typewriter, and green mould was float-ing in a half-empty coffee cup.

Wisting opened the curtains to let in more light. Across the street, where the Salvation Army premises were located, two men were carrying a fund-raising container out to a car.

He sat down and drew the chair up to the desk, trying it out for size, testing the springs and swaying slightly from side to side. There was a family photograph on the desk in front of him. He knew that the man in the picture had been suspended on suspicion of theft from the evidence store, but this was something no one spoke about. Officially, he was on long-term sick leave.

The sheet of paper in the typewriter was the beginning of a report concerning an inspection of dealers in second hand goods. Wisting removed it and laid it aside.

He spent quarter of an hour writing notes. No matter how he worded them, the content ended up seeming inconsequential. Everything grew insignificant on a typewritten sheet.

Pulling out the paper, he smoothed it out and signed under-neath. One of the experienced investigators walking along the corridor stopped, took a step back, and gave him a questioning look.

'I'm just borrowing a typewriter,' Wisting explained.

The detective shrugged and walked on. Wisting took the blue file, Norway's internal police directory, from the shelf before him and leafed through to find the number for Oslo police district's traffic section.

A man's grumpy voice answered, and Wisting gave his name and police station. 'I'm not sure if you're the right person to speak to, but I'm trying to find the owner of an old car.'

'Then you'll have to contact the Driver and Vehicle Licensing Agency,' the man replied.

'I'm talking about a vintage car. From the time when police kept records of chassis numbers.'

'I've no idea what you're talking about,' the other man said. 'But I know who you should speak to – Arne Vikene. He has a vintage car himself, and is a member of the Police Historical Society.'

Wisting made a note of the name. 'Could you transfer me to him, please?'

'He works in administration. I can transfer you to the switchboard and you can ask for him there.'

Wisting thanked him and waited while the phone rang. After some to-ing and fro-ing, he reached the appropriate office, where he learned that Arne Vikene was off duty, but would be back the following day. He was given a direct number and expressed his appreciation for their help. Carrying his sheaf of notes, he closed the door behind him.

Dokken was sitting in his office with the phone at his ear and a cigarette in his mouth. Nodding, he pointed to the bundle of tip-offs in the blue tray as he continued to talk on the phone. Wisting put down the sheet of paper. Shifting the phone receiver to his other ear, Dokken picked up the memo and moved it to the bottom of the pile without looking at it.

9

By half past three, Wisting had returned to the barn and parked his car beside the black, charred tree trunks. With their sprawling branches, and in the fading daylight, they conjured up an eerie and unnerving atmosphere. He took Rupert's flashlight from the back of the car.

He entered through the barn doors, pulling them shut again as soon as he was inside. He pointed the flashlight beam at the chain on the floor. This padlock was not as rusty as the one on the outside, but it had been sheltered from wind and rain.

From a purely theoretical point of view, it would have been possible to thread the chain through the bolts on the inside while the doors were open, and pull the chain taut while closing them again. You could then rotate the key in the padlock from outside when the doors were almost shut and push the lock and the remaining chain through the narrow gap between the doors before they shut fast.

No matter that it was possible to lock the doors on both sides, it still made no sense.

If he had been a detective examining a crime scene, he would have placed the chain and padlock in an evidence bag. Instead, he left them untouched.

He went to the filthy mattress. Mice had been nibbling at it. The damage looked like frayed bullet holes after a hail of gunshots.

The newspaper at one end was a copy of *Verdens Gang* for 24 July 1973. The front-page splash was the story of a Palestinian liberation group that had hijacked a Boeing aircraft *en route* between Amsterdam and Tokyo. The journey had ended in Libya, where the terrorists freed the hostages and blew up the plane.

That was ten years before, when Wisting had been at the start of his teens. He vaguely remembered hearing about the incident.

Beside the newspaper were a couple of issues of *Kriminaljournalen,* a true-crime magazine aimed at a mainly male readership. The front pages were in colour, with pictures of scantily clad women. One of them contained, among other things, an interview with the celebrity lawyer Alf Nordhus in addition to accounts of real-life crime dramas.

Wisting glanced at the barn doors. The magazines were not pornographic, but exciting enough to entertain teenagers in the seventies. The mattress could have been left behind by boys who had played in the barn in the same way that Knut Heian had done in the thirties. That could explain the padlock on the inside of the doors.

Laying aside the magazines, he discovered a grey rucksack jammed between a milk churn and a wooden packing case. Something sticky brushed against his ear when he crouched to remove it: a spider's web laden with dead flies that he swept away with his hand.

A stale smell arrived with the bag as he pulled it towards him. In a cavity behind its hiding place was a pair of brown boots with the tops turned down. He lifted them out and noted they were worn, almost entirely ruined, with lopsided heels and holes in the leather.

The rucksack had three exterior pockets, one on either side and one in the centre at the front. In the left pocket, he found a screwdriver, pincers and a knife. The other side pocket was empty. In the middle pocket he found a white, sealed envelope addressed to *Anna* in sloping letters.

He weighed up whether to open it and decided it was better to leave as much as possible untouched, so he put it back.

The large compartment in the rucksack held a sweater, a shirt, a pair of thick socks and a pair of trousers.

As he packed everything into the bag again, he noticed that it was marked with a name, at the top of the interior flap, and written with a black felt-tip pen. The first name was Alfred, but the surname was more difficult to make out. The dampness had caused the letters to run, but to his mind it looked like either Danielsen or Davidsen.

He returned the rucksack and shone the flashlight around to search for any other belongings that might have been left behind, or signs that might tell him more about the person who had been holed up in the barn.

A noise on the eastern wall made him stiffen. He switched off the flashlight and stood still, listening. Streaks of grey winter light filtered in through gaps in the wall planks. A shadow of something on the move caused the dim light to change shape. Again he heard the noise, and it took some time for him to realise that it was only the wind rushing through the trees outside. The strongest gusts scraped against the walls and roof.

He switched on the flashlight once more. A dead pigeon lay on the floor, its legs in the air – all that was left of it was fragile bones and bluish-grey feathers.

Stepping over the bird, he lifted the mattress on its side to peer underneath. The dark earthen floor was covered in tracks made by insects that had burrowed through passages and tunnels. Two dried-out, grey beetles lay squashed on the ground.

He was about to put the mattress down again when he discovered a key. It was almost completely caked in earth, so he had to dig it out. Small and flat, when he rubbed it between his fingers to clean it, he found a brown encrustation that he was unable to remove, no matter how hard he tried.

It struck him that this must be the key for the padlock. He crossed to the barn doors, where he retrieved the chain and tried. It slid in easily. However, the lock had been so badly damaged by Knut Heian's axe that he could not turn the key.

He threw down the padlock and chain with the key still inside.

A massive truck passed on the road outside. It was past four o'clock now and he was hungry. Ingrid would be wondering what had become of him.

Directing the light at the old car at the far end of the barn, he picked his way through the debris. Clearing enough space to move it out of here would be a major task when the time came.

Motes of dust danced around him as he pulled the tarpaulin halfway to one side, so that he could study the bullet hole again.

It was almost one centimetre in diameter, indicating a relatively high calibre gun. The percussion power also suggested that. The bullet had traversed the bodywork and entered the back of the rear seat. The vehicle would have to be dismantled to remove it: only then could they ascertain what kind of ammunition they were dealing with.

He opened the car and sat inside. The rear seat was shaped like a settee. It was slightly uneven, but far from uncomfortable.

A newspaper jutted from a pocket in the back of the seat in front of him. Wisting drew it out, his interest piqued. This might give a clue about when the car had been stowed in the barn.

It was a copy of *Aftenposten* dated 17 August 1925, nearly sixty years before. Most of the front page was given over to an account of an ongoing rail strike. *Supplies of beef and pork for Kristiania are beginning to become scarce.* Roald Amundsen was preparing an expedition to the North Pole in an airship, he read, and there was a lengthy article about German reparations following the First World War.

Of greatest interest was the date. It was likely that the newspaper had been fairly hot-off-the-press when the car had set out on its final trip.

He replaced the newspaper and moved to the front passenger seat to look in the glove compartment. He opened it, hoping to find a registration card or other vehicle documents, but all he found was a pair of dark leather gloves. However, just as he was closing it, he spotted something else: a hole at the front of the side door. Its shape and size were very similar to the bullet hole in the rear wing.

Opening the door, he stepped out and attempted to find the entry hole. He had to rub off moss and other deposits to locate it. The shot had entered the bodywork diagonally, two metres farther forward from the bullet hole at the back, as if the vehicle had been shot at twice while in motion.

He sat inside the car again and tried to work out what had happened to the bullet. The front seat was in an even worse state than the one in the rear. It was discoloured and torn. To determine the exact trajectory of the bullet, he went out to fetch a metal tube he had spotted on the shelves of tools. Its circumference was slightly smaller than the bullet hole, and as he guided it carefully through the opening, he visualised how the gunman must have been hiding in a ditch, below road level.

The tube emerged on the inside of the cabin. He continued to push until almost all of it was inside, before sitting in the driving seat to follow the sight line. The tube pointed directly at the driver, but there was no hole in the back of the seat.

The bullet must have hit whoever was sitting in the driver's seat, at chest height, and come to a sudden stop inside his body.

10

Wisting should have gone home to Ingrid and the twins, but it crossed his mind that he might call in at the library first. What Rupert had said about King Haakon had been at the back of his mind all along. The former king had driven an old Minerva that had probably been scrapped. *At least, nobody knows what became of it*, Rupert had said.

He parked beside Skottebrygga and set off towards the tower block where the town's public library was housed.

Having no idea where he should begin his search, he joined the queue at the front desk. Two elderly women were in front of him. One of them was borrowing a dog-eared book by Dag Solstad. Ingrid had a copy at home, but Wisting had never read it. It was about a teacher at Larvik High School who had been drawn into the Workers' Communist Party. The other woman was holding a translated book that had been recently filmed. He recognised the title from the cinema hoardings.

When they had their library cards stamped, it was Wisting's turn. 'I'm looking for a book about King Haakon,' he said. 'Could you help me with that?'

'There are several,' the librarian answered. 'Is there anything in particular you're interested in?'

'His cars.'

She gave him a slightly curious look before leading him to the Biography shelves where she took out a book with a reddish cover and the king's monogram on the spine.

'This is a relatively new biography,' she said, handing it to him. 'Do you have a library card?'

'I don't have it with me.'

The librarian sighed.

'Can I get a new one?'

'Not if you've just forgotten to bring yours with you.'

'I could sit down and leaf through it, and then I could come back and borrow it tomorrow,' he suggested.

She nodded her assent.

An old man glanced up from his newspaper when Wisting sat in a vacant chair at one of the tables. The bank raid was still prominent on the front pages.

It did not take Wisting long to find a picture of the king's first motor car, with the registration number A1. The quality of the photograph was poor, but, as far as he could see, it was identical to the car in the barn.

The king had obtained a driving licence in 1913, he read. After that he acquired not just one but, in fact, two cars, one open-top and the other a saloon-type, to drive depending on the weather. Both were from the Belgian Minerva marque.

The car was mainly used between the Royal Palace and the king's estate on Bygdøy, but it was also used on longer trips. In the saloon he had travelled to Fagernes and Nordland among other places.

Wisting skimmed the text, curious to know what had become of the royal vehicles. The king was described as a careful driver, but it stated that he was annoyed that the speed limit in Kristiania was only fifteen kilometres an hour.

He could find nothing about what had happened to the cars, and continued to leaf through the book to see if there was an index. He found what he was looking for in the list of photographs. The picture of King Haakon's Minerva had been loaned by Tynset Museum and Historical Society and taken during a private visit in July 1926.

If the copy of *Aftenposten* dated Monday 17 August 1925 was dated accurately, it could not be the king's car that was stashed away with a bullet hole in the barn at Tveidalen.

The man opposite folded his newspaper and put it down.

Wisting brought his book to the front desk, where another thought struck him.

'Do you have old copies of *Østlands-Posten*?' he asked.

'Which year?' the librarian asked.

'1925.'

'Then it'll be on microfilm,' she said. 'I can set you up for an hour tomorrow, if you do want to come back and borrow the book.'

Wisting told her that he no longer needed it, but would appreciate looking at the newspapers from the summer of 1925. The librarian promised to look them out and reserve a microfilm reader for ten o'clock the next day.

Ingrid was out of sorts when he returned home. The twins had been awake for long periods, and she had not managed to do anything she had planned.

'And where did you take yourself?' she asked. 'I'd arranged to meet Mona at six o'clock. I won't make it now.'

Wisting dashed his hand against his forehead. He had been so absorbed that he had entirely forgotten his home life.

'Sorry,' he said, feeling guilty. He appreciated that the days could drag on your own with two small children, and he really ought to have eased the load in his off-duty hours. 'I promise to pull my weight in future. It's just that I got so engrossed.'

'It's okay,' she said, but in a dejected tone. 'I've let Mona know. We'll meet up nearer Christmas.'

He ate the leftovers from dinner and tried to read the newspaper with Line on his lap while Thomas slept. She kept punching the paper, babbling something unintelligible all the while, so he ended up reading out loud. The gentle, rhythmic sound of his voice persuaded her to sit quietly.

It was still too early to determine the sum the bank robbers had made off with, but it was obviously millions of kroner. The newspaper also carried an interview with the owner of the stolen black Sierra who said that the car had been taken while he was working night shift at the chemicals factory. Apart from those minor details, it seemed as if all trace of the perpetrators had come to a halt at the burned out car in Tveidalen. The theory about the criminal gang in Oslo was clearly something that the investigators had no wish to publicise.

He read to the end of the article, but noticed that his initial interest in the case had waned, overshadowed to some extent by what had occurred on a late summer's day in 1925.

Line grew restless again when he folded the newspaper and stopped reading, but settled when he placed her in the playpen beside her brother.

In the room where he slept in the afternoons, and where Ingrid had a desk she used for correcting schoolwork, he sat and began to jot down keywords about what he knew and what questions were still open. The more he got things down, the clearer it became to him that the old car in the barn did not merely represent an unsolved mystery, but probably also an undetected crime.

11

More snow fell overnight; wet, heavy snow that Wisting spent an hour clearing from his front steps and driveway.

The roads into town had been snowploughed badly, which slowed his drive to work. After struggling to find a parking spot, he had to walk two blocks to the police station.

A notice had been pinned on the duty roster assigning overtime shifts, mostly night shifts. Wisting checked for his own entries and filled in his name wherever he found a space.

Itching to sit in the empty office in CID, he instead installed himself in the report room downstairs near the front desk.

Arne Vikene, in Oslo Police District's administration department, answered almost at once. Wisting could hear from his voice that he was getting on in years.

He explained that he was trying to trace the owner of a vintage car, and had learned that Vikene was the very man to help.

Arne Vikene's interest was aroused. 'What kind of car is it?'

'A Belgian Minerva.' Wisting replied like an expert. 'Probably imported between 1915 and 1925.'

'There aren't many of those left,' Vikene said.

'It's been stored in a barn for almost sixty years.'

'Sixty years! What's the owner of the barn got to say about it?'

'The car was already there when he inherited the barn. I'm trying to help him find out whether its owner is still alive.'

'What sort of condition is it in?'

'Pretty bad.' Wisting hoped to avoid making him too interested. 'It was damaged in a collision and has been destroyed by damp.'

Vikene asked a number of questions about the car, and

Wisting responded to the best of his ability before returning to the reason for his call. 'I have the engine and chassis numbers for the vehicle. Could you help me find out more about it?'

'I know where the records are stored,' Vikene said. 'But they can be difficult to search through if you don't know the name of the owner or the registration number.'

'Surely there's also a register of chassis numbers?'

'Yes, that's true,' Vikene agreed. 'Chassis numbers, factory brand names, year of manufacture, total number of seats, number of cylinders, axle pressure ... everything's there, in chronological order.'

They agreed that Vikene would search through the records and fax Wisting a copy of whatever he managed to track down. 'I can do it later today,' he said.

Wisting logged the conversation before leafing through the telephone book to find Knut Heian's phone number.

'Have you discovered anything else?' the farmer asked.

'I'm working on it. A name has cropped up and I wondered if you were familiar with it.'

'Fire away.'

'Alfred.'

'Just Alfred, nothing more?'

'Could be Danielsen or Davidsen. Does that mean anything to you?'

Knut Heian took time to mull this over, before confirming that the name was unknown to him.

'What about Anna?'

Heian said he had a distant relative called Anna. Wisting did not think this would be the right person, but noted her name in full and concluded the conversation before Heian could ask how these names had come to light.

The snow delayed him and he arrived ten minutes late for his appointment with the microfilm reader at the library. The librarian he had spoken to the previous day was absent, but another woman located his appointment in a book.

'You're late,' she pointed out, as she rose from behind the counter.

Making no comment, Wisting followed her into the local history section where two reading devices with advanced optical equipment, a mirror and a large screen were set up. None of them appeared to have been used for some time.

'Have you used microfilm before?' she asked, as she took a roll of film from a metal storage tin.

Wisting shook his head. She mounted the film in the apparatus and showed him how to navigate through it. He quickly got the hang of it and soon old newspaper pages were sliding across the screen until he reached September 1925. The main story here was a report of the opening match at the new grass football pitch at Lovisenlund Stadium. Larvik Turn, the local team, had beaten Fram 1-0.

The newspaper in the old car was dated 17 August 1925. He spooled back and found his way to Tuesday 18 August of that year, without being entirely sure what he was trying to find.

The paper featured the current rail strike, but also reported prominently on Roald Amundsen's bankruptcy. Creditors in Alaska had confiscated the polar vessel, *Maud*, which had been trapped in ice in the Bering Strait for three winters.

He ran his eye over the pages and found what he was searching for: Oscar Wisting. His great-grandfather's name virtually shone out at him from the newspaper page on the screen. He had been a member of the expedition, and Wisting wondered if this was the closest anyone in his family had come to fame.

He browsed further, reading the headlines, but found nothing of interest.

In the next edition, he noticed a story about a traffic accident in Storgata. A woman had been knocked down by a 'motorised bicycle', breaking her right forearm and 'damaging her hip'. Two days later, another accident had occurred. In heavy rain, the service bus from Fredriksvern naval base had collided with a car on the corner of Dronningens gate and Kristian Fredriks vei. One of the passengers had sprained his hand, but both vehicles had been able to drive on after the incident.

It had obviously been a hot summer. There were warnings about the great danger of forest fires, and prognostications that the drought would have severe consequences for the potato and grain harvests. He smiled to himself at the sight of the old advertisements, but found no news that could possibly relate to the vintage car in the barn.

Leaning back in his chair, he stared absentmindedly through the window. Squalls from the sea lashed the pane with snow that melted and trickled down the glass.

The vehicle need not be local, he thought. It could have been in transit. *Aftenposten* was chiefly an Oslo newspaper in 1925, and the main road south from Oslo passes through Larvik.

He spooled back the microfilm, replacing it in the metal tin, and handed it in at the front desk. 'Do you have *Aftenposten* on microfilm?' he asked.

'Not here, I'm afraid,' the librarian said, 'but we can order it from the National Library.'

Wisting gave this some thought. He was reluctant to make unnecessary work, but when the librarian asked whether they should order it, he accepted and said what year he was interested in.

'I'll phone in the order,' she said, glancing at the clock. 'If you're lucky, we'll have it here by the weekend.'

12

On his way home, Wisting popped into the local shop and bought several items on a list Ingrid had given him. Afterwards they cooked dinner together, pork chops with gravy and potatoes. The atmosphere between them had improved since Ingrid had managed a couple of hours' sleep during the day, and the feeding had gone smoothly. They talked about how they planned to celebrate Christmas. They had invited both sets of parents to dinner on Christmas Eve, and this was something they were looking forward to.

'What would you like for Christmas?' Ingrid asked.

He prodded his fork into a piece of potato and moved it towards his mouth. 'I don't know. Maybe some new clothes.'

'They'll be cheaper in the January sales,' Ingrid said. 'There must be something else you'd like.'

He could not think of anything and, really, there was nothing he needed. 'What about you?' he asked.

Ingrid shook her head. 'Perhaps we shouldn't buy each other anything this year. We have the children to think of, after all, and they're going to need lots more things soon.'

Wisting didn't reply. He knew that Ingrid would find something for him whatever they agreed now.

'I've volunteered for some overtime shifts.'

Ingrid nodded, as aware as he was that they needed the extra money. At the same time, she wanted to have him at home as much as possible.

He pondered whether to tell Ingrid about the private investigation he was conducting, but decided to hold back. He knew that he really ought to spend his free time at home with his wife

60

and children, and that this continual absence would not bring more money into his pay packet.

Afterwards, he tackled the washing up, wondering whether to go outside to clear the snow before having a snooze. He decided to do it immediately before setting off for his stint of night duty.

He gave Ingrid a goodnight kiss before heading into the workroom and closing the door behind him. Before he lay down he sat at the desk and riffled through the Minerva notes, thinking that sooner or later he would have to approach Ove Dokken with his discoveries. It could concern a murder, and at some time or other the investigation would have to be elevated to an official footing. However, he had no wish to submit another memo, only to have it land at the bottom of a heap.

Before he took any further steps, he decided to complete as thorough a preliminary investigation as possible. The car had been hidden in the barn for almost sixty years. Whatever had taken place had become time-barred long ago, and the participants were probably no longer living. A few more days would not matter much.

When he got up a few hours later, Ingrid had gone to bed. Yet another layer of snow had enveloped the previous one, and he went outside to clear the driveway before having a shower and getting dressed for work.

He left early, hoping that a fax from Arne Vikene with information from the old vehicle records would be waiting for him in his pigeonhole. All he found there was a list of the extra shifts he had been allocated. Three tours of night duty, the first of these the very next night, meaning that not only would he have to work a double shift, but also he would be paid extra, money that would certainly come in handy.

'Early tonight?' asked the officer going off duty.

'Did a fax come for me, by any chance?'

'For you?' The Duty Sergeant pulled his glasses down from his forehead.

'From Oslo.'

The Duty Sergeant took out a book with a stiff, green cover in which all ingoing and outgoing faxes were logged. His finger ran down the lines.

'Maybe it's been sent to CID by mistake,' he suggested, glancing upwards.

'Maybe.'

Wisting headed for the stairs.

The fluorescent tube in the ceiling buzzed, and then the light began to flicker before the whole corridor in the Criminal Investigation Department was flooded with harsh light.

The fax machine was located in the records office, and a red light was flashing: *Paper empty*.

Taking a step inside the photocopy room, he found a stack of A4 paper. He had never filled the machine before, and fumbled around a bit before he managed to open the drawer. The red light went out, but apart from that, nothing happened when he slid the drawer back. As he was about to leave, the machine began to tick over.

Wisting went back to check the sheet of paper on its way out, and saw that *Oslo Police District – Administration Department* was given as the sender, and that this was *Page 1 of 3*.

The first page simply identified Arne Vikene, but the next page was a copy of a handwritten record. The letters were small and neat, although ink stains from the rollers in the machine made it difficult to read.

He waited until the third sheet emerged before taking the printout with him to the office he had used the previous day. It was unlocked.

He left the overhead light switched off, but sat down at the desk and turned on the lamp. Yellow light cast a circle in front of him.

Arne Vikene had located the right car. Both the chassis and engine numbers agreed with Wisting's notes. It was a Minerva Saloon with four doors and twenty-horse power, imported via

Oslo Harbour on 17 June 1920. The owner was the Kristiania Haulage Company. The name and title of a contact person was listed: Martinius Bergan, haulier. The registration number allocated to the vehicle was A795. Near the foot of the page, a comment was added but had faded and was impossible to read.

The third sheet was a copy of the ownership records, with a list of all the cars belonging to the Kristiania Haulage Company. Every one appeared to have been sold off, and the names of the new owners were recorded. A795 was mentioned around the middle of the page, and in the column concerning the sale and new owner, he saw the following comment: *Lost, 21.08.1925.*

Wisting leaned back in his chair. 'Lost,' he said aloud to himself. It was a strange choice of words. Not stolen or missing, but lost. Gone.

The date coincided with the newspaper he had found inside the car, dated four days prior to the car being regarded as lost.

To make further progress, he would have to talk to someone connected to the Kristiania Haulage Company, or else get hold of descendants of the contact person listed on the form.

He wrote down the name: Martinius Bergan.

Kristiania Haulage Company could be a courier firm, or a forerunner of Transportsentralen, the present-day major distribution, transport and haulage company.

Folding the fax in two, he slipped it inside his notebook before switching off the desk lamp and leaving the room.

The door to the Chief Inspector's office was open. Wisting stepped inside to check the tray of tip-offs, and found that not only had the pile reduced, but also his own memo was no longer there. On a nearby sideboard he found a separate in-tray for new documents. He thumbed through them and noticed that most dealt with routine investigations, such as interviews with bank employees and conversations with people who had observed what they thought were suspicious persons and vehicles.

Almost at the bottom of the pile, he found a report about investigations into holiday cottage H292. Wisting felt a frisson of excitement, pleased that the information he had contributed to the case had been taken seriously and investigated further.

He had to sit down to read it. The report writer had been in contact with Vivian Brun, co-owner of the cottage with her husband, Roger. They lived in Oslo, and had not visited their cottage since September. She had no idea who could have been there last weekend, but a nephew with a talent for joinery work, and who lived in Larvik, had taken on renewing the fascia and exterior cladding of the south-facing wall. This was during the autumn. She did not know whether the work was completed.

The report writer had followed up by phoning the nephew, who said he had postponed the straightforward job several times, but that last weekend he and a friend had finally begun. They had used a key left in an arranged spot, but had started by having a few beers. Not much had been achieved on the first day. The following day, they had been surprised by the snow, and had had left with the work unfinished. The renovation would now have to wait until spring.

Wisting read the document twice, and made a note of the nephew's name: Jens Brun. The name of the friend who had been with him was not given. Neither had any control questions been posed about when they had arrived and when they had left.

The explanation was plausible but, before Wisting put back the report, he underlined the name of the nephew in his note-book with two emphatic strokes.

Erling Storvolden had taken over the duty desk when Wisting returned downstairs, and sat sorting through some papers.

'Do we have a phone catalogue for Oslo?' Wisting asked.

Storvolden turned to the wall and selected the correct directory. 'It's a few years old,' he said. 'I usually just phone Directory Enquiries.'

Wisting opened the catalogue at the letter B and found more listings for Bergan than he had anticipated, running from the foot of one column to the middle of the next. There was a Martin, but no Martinius. He had not really expected to find one, anyway. If Martinius Bergan had been a grown man in 1925, he was probably no longer living.

He took the directory with him to the photocopy machine and copied the page. It was too late to start phoning round, so he folded the sheet and inserted it into his notebook alongside the fax.

He liked to take these small steps that steadily brought him closer to an answer. This was what investigation was all about.

13

The night hours crawled by without much happening. They patrolled the deserted streets, stopped a car with a broken headlight and checked on an elderly woman who was driving erratically.

Just after one o'clock they received a report about a man who had climbed a ladder and broken through a window on the first floor of a house in Valby. It turned out that the man in question was the householder who had locked himself out.

Around two it stopped snowing, and the weather improved for a few hours before snow began to fall again.

At three o'clock they showed up in the patrol car to monitor the car park outside the chemicals factory. After staring at the wintry night for half an hour, Per Haugen began to snore. Thirty minutes later, a tractor equipped with a snowplough appeared to clear the area around the factory. Haugen suggested that they should drive back, and sat dozing in a chair until their shift was over.

Wisting had to clear a space in front of the house before he could park. By then, Ingrid and the twins had already been up for a few hours. He could see that she had not managed much sleep that night either.

'You go and lie down again,' he said. 'Take the bed settee.'

'What about you?'

He shook his head. He was keen to make as good an impression as possible at work, which did mean he had to be in good shape, but not at Ingrid's expense.

'I'll go to bed too, as soon as they're asleep.'

Making no protest, she cleared away the breakfast dishes before closing the door behind her.

Wisting buttered a slice of bread and ate while watching the two babies in the playpen. Thomas lay chewing his fists, while Line played with a plastic toy.

He took out his investigation notes. While he was at Police College, he had looked forward to going out on patrol. The first few weeks had lived up to his expectations: there was a certain excitement in never knowing what was going to happen and what a spell of duty might involve. Now though, he longed to move on and away from shift work, from getting up as other people were going to bed. He wanted to work in an office where he could make a real effort to do something about crime, not simply trail along at the back once something had occurred.

An hour later, the twins were sleepy. He lifted them up, one at a time, and laid them in their cots in the bedroom. He was leaning in to kiss Thomas on the forehead and tuck the blanket round him when, suddenly, the room began to spin. The dizziness lasted no more than a second. As he used the wall for support, it brought home to him how tired he was.

He undressed and crept silently under the quilt, aware that his body did not benefit from this changing daily rhythm. Even though he was tired, he had difficulty sleeping. Tossing and turning, for some reason his mind dwelled on the man who had locked himself out and climbed in through the window. Something about it rankled, and it kept him awake. His thoughts forged ahead, ending up where they had often done in recent days: back at the barn at Tveidalskrysset.

Knut Heian had spoken of how, as a boy, he had climbed in and out of the barn by pulling a ladder up through the opening in the north wall. Wisting had walked around the barn and peered in through the gaps before the snow had fallen. There had been no ladder outside the barn. However, on the inside there had been an old wooden ladder, with fishing nets and glass floats dangling from the treads. That could be the same ladder but, if the ladder was inside the barn, how had Alfred got out?

The barn door was locked on the inside, and the only alternative exit was the opening high on the wall. That turned the old barn into a locked room.

His thoughts churned as sleep closed in. Half in dreams, he visited the barn again, picturing in his mind's eye the mattress, the old newspaper, the rucksack with the letter to Anna, and the worn-out boots. Dusty folding chairs, rusty tools, cobwebs, paint tins, car tyres, corrugated metal, potato crates and thick ropes hanging from roof beams.

Just before he dropped off, the solution came creeping up on him. Whoever this Alfred was who had slept on the mattress, he was still somewhere inside the barn.

14

Wisting woke with a sense of unease at half past one, two and a half hours before the double shift. First the evening shift, and then overtime.

Propped on his elbows, he looked across at the cots. Ingrid must have come in to fetch the twins without him waking. He lay down and reconsidered the deduction he had made before falling asleep. It did not seem so clear cut now, but all the same it possessed a certain logic. What, obviously, counted against it was that they had not found a corpse inside the barn. If Alfred had ended his days in there, the most natural thing would have been for them to find him lying on the mattress. Of course, the body could be hidden, but whoever had done the hiding would also have been unable to get out. The most obvious explanation would be that Alfred had taken his own life. The unsent letter to Anna might be a letter of farewell.

A note from Ingrid lay on the kitchen table: *At Ellen's*. Ellen was a friend from school who had a son three months older than the twins.

He carried his thoughts outside and cleared away the last layer of snow. His idea that there was a corpse inside the barn grew more distant as he worked. The most plausible explanation was that there had been another ladder that had later been removed.

Ingrid drove up when he had finished clearing the snow. He helped her out of the car with the twins. Thomas had fallen asleep, but Line was wide-awake and wide-eyed.

As they ate at the table, he told Ingrid about the bullet holes in the car and the information he had gathered about the owner. He simply had to share these thoughts with someone.

Ingrid put down her fork. 'Bullet holes! It must have been something serious. You have to go on with this.'

'I'm too much away from you and the children as it is. This is almost certainly something I'll have to investigate in my free time, as I've been doing up till now.'

Ingrid gave this some thought.

'We're fine,' she said. 'Just stick to our arrangements and help when you're here. You know, I like it when you get so enthusiastic it's impossible for you to let things lie.'

Wisting smiled, aware of how lucky he was. It was a common subject in conversations with his colleagues that their wives complained about them being so seldom at home.

'You must do something with it,' she said. 'Go and speak to some of the detectives.'

'I'll do that eventually,' Wisting said, 'but right now they're all engrossed in the bank robbery. I'll find out a bit more before I broach it with them.'

It was just after three o'clock, barely an hour before he had to return to work, but he had time to phone some of the names on the list of people with the surname Bergan.

He took the phone cable with him into the workroom and shut the door.

Anders Bergan was the first, but there was no reply. The next one was *Bjørn Bergan*, who seemed annoyed. Wisting explained who he was and asked if the other man knew of someone called Martinius Bergan.

'Why are you asking?'

''I'm looking for somebody whose name was given as a contact for the Kristiania Haulage Company in 1925,' Wisting said.

'In 1925?'

'Yes, it's about a vintage car.'

'I've no knowledge of anything like that.'

Wisting repeated that he was trying to track down Martinius

Bergan but, after a few more exchanges, he was able to strike Bjørn Bergan from his list.

In the next two phone conversations, questions and answers went to and fro in similar fashion before he could score out another couple of names.

The fourth person he rang was called Erik. Wisting introduced himself and added that he worked for the police in Larvik. That meant no questions were asked about why he was phoning. Erik Bergan gave straightforward answers and told him that he had never heard of anyone called Martinius in his family.

He managed to call another two before it was time to go to work.

The first few hours flew by, taken up with minor tasks. Someone had been throwing icy snowballs and broken a window at Mesterfjellet School. The ferry from Denmark had reported an extremely intoxicated passenger who had to be extricated from underneath a staircase and arrested for being drunk and disorderly. Two boys had broken into the area behind the fences at the Farris factory and stolen empty bottles. Footprints in the snow led straight to the bottle depository in the shop along the street.

At seven o'clock they drove back to have a bite to eat and write their reports. Wisting brought his lunchbox with him into the workroom and filled out the forms while he ate one of his sandwiches. When he had finished, he closed the door and took out the phone list. He rang Halvor and Halfdan, with no result, but Geir Bergan did recognise the name.

'My grandfather was called Martinius,' he said.

Wisting's grip on his pen grew tighter. 'Is he alive?'

'No, but my grandmother is.'

'What's her name?'

'Ragna. She lives at Veitvet.'

'Would it be possible to phone her?'

'She's got a phone, but she's a bit deaf. I don't think you'd

71

get much out of her. You'd be better speaking to my father.'

Wisting asked for his name and phone number and made a note of Jan Bergan at Kalbakken. He thanked Geir for his help and dialled the number.

Jan Bergan's voice was deep and husky, as if he smoked too many cigarettes. Wisting introduced himself and explained that his son had given his name and number. 'I'm looking for descendants of the Martinius Bergan who was connected to the Kristiania Haulage Company.'

The man at the other end cleared his throat. 'That sounds like my father,' he replied. 'What's this about?'

'I'm trying to locate the owner of an old car.'

'What kind of car?' The voice had changed, the tone more guarded.

'A vintage car from 1925. The records show that it was reported missing in 1925.'

Wisting could hear the man breathing faster. 'Have you found it?'

'Apparently so.'

'What about Marvin and the money?'

Wisting moved the phone receiver from one ear to the other. 'What do you mean?'

'Have you found Marvin and the money?' Jan Bergan repeated.

'No, just the car,' Wisting said, 'but there are circumstances about the discovery that I'd like to talk to you about.'

'I was no more than three at that time,' Bergan said. 'I don't know much about it.'

'What about your mother?'

'This business of the car wasn't something that was talked about much.'

'Now that it's been found,' Wisting ventured, 'do you think she might be interested in arriving at some sort of resolution?'

'You should really come here,' Bergan said.

Wisting recalled what his duty roster looked like. 'I can come tomorrow afternoon,' he said.

72

The workroom door opened and Per Haugen waved at him: 'Road accident!'

Wisting hurriedly concluded the arrangement to meet Jan Bergan and his mother at four o'clock the following day before dashing out to the patrol car.

Haugen was already behind the steering wheel with the engine idling. 'Head-on collision on the E18.'

Wisting pulled a face. Front collisions on the motorway were always serious. The stretch of road through the Larvik police district was one of the most vulnerable in the network and had claimed the lives of four victims already that year.

The traffic ahead was at a standstill and they struggled to inch forward through the driving snow. Fire and ambulance services were already on the scene. Wisting leapt out and tried to gain an overview of the situation. It looked as though an Opel Ascona had skidded into the oncoming lane and hit a Mazda, one of the newer models. Two of the injured were already on stretchers, with another two left in the wrecked cars. The front-seat passenger in the Ascona was trapped inside and screaming in pain while the fire crew worked to cut him free. The driver of the Mazda appeared lifeless, with the steering wheel and instrument panel compressing his ribcage.

It took half an hour to transport the injured to hospital and leave the accident scene to the police and the salvage company workers.

Wisting took witness statements and photographs, made a note of registration numbers and sketched out the location of the vehicles before the cars were taken away and the debris removed.

He spent the rest of the evening shift writing reports. An elderly couple from Skien were the occupants of the Mazda, and two friends from Horten had been travelling in the Ascona. The hospital reported that the man in the Mazda had been declared dead on arrival at Accident and Emergency. His wife had escaped with a broken arm.

The driver of the Ascona had received minor injuries, but his companion had sustained serious head wounds. Wisting transcribed the information to the report form before extracting it from the typewriter.

He sat with the form in his hands pondering on how grim, dramatic events turned into sober words when committed to paper, and reflected on whether this was what his life in the police force would be like. Momentous episodes for individual people would become a routine part of his everyday life.

On the night shift, he was paired with Eivind Larsen, a conscientious police officer almost twenty years his senior. Wisting was behind the wheel of the patrol car when they drove into the night.

Their first assignment concerned a bus that had skidded and become stuck in a snowdrift, forcing traffic to be redirected while a tow truck hauled it out. The next report was about a chimney fire in Langestrand. Around restaurant closing time they had to break up a fight outside the premises of Otto På Torget; and at 01.40 they had to take care of a drunk man who had fallen asleep on the train from Oslo.

After all the report writing and a quick snack, Eivind Larsen took over the driving seat.

'I understood you noticed a pattern,' Larsen said, as they drove to the east end of town.

Wisting did not immediately understand what he meant.

'The car thefts,' Larsen said. 'What do the statistics look like for Thursday nights?'

'Sunday nights and Thursday nights stand out.'

'What do you say to us trying to put a stop to it?'

'I'm in.'

They found a different surveillance post that afforded an equally good view of the car park in front of the chemicals factory. For the first half hour, they sat in silence.

'Have you ever thought of becoming a detective?' Wisting asked.

Eivind Larsen shook his head. 'That's not up my street. Having things hanging over your head all the time. I like to go home and relax when the working day is over, and not have constant responsibility and the weight of expectation resting on my shoulders. In the uniformed branch you can write a report about what you've done and what you've seen, and then your job is over. The detectives look after the rest, and they never have time off. We're the ones who have all the fun.'

Wisting could not quite follow his train of thought. What lay behind the crime was what interested him. It was not sufficient to observe and record what had happened. He wanted to unearth more answers and not merely uncover what had taken place. Who was behind it and why did they do what they had done? There was a certain satisfaction in continually moving closer to a solution, almost the same as filling in a crossword when the answers began to intersect and lead to fewer blank spaces. He liked to reveal secrets and expose things that had been kept quiet.

His thoughts slipped back to the old car in the barn and his forthcoming meeting with Martinius Bergan's widow. What she might be able to recall brought with it a feeling he had not experienced for a long time, a tingling sensation in the pit of his stomach reminiscent of hunger.

'Over there!' Eivind Larsen said, before dropping his voice: 'Two o'clock.'

Diagonally in front of them was a man in dark clothing with a small rucksack on his back and his hands deep inside his jacket pockets.

In the shadow between the light shed by two streetlamps, he stopped and surveyed his surroundings. He was too far away for them to notice any distinguishing features.

Neither said anything. The man continued walking.

Twenty metres farther on, a Corolla was parked with a fox's tail dangling from the radio antenna. The man slowed down and looked around again when he was level with the vehicle, before hunkering down and peering into the car.

Wisting grabbed the portable radio, thrust open the car door and stepped outside. Snow crunched under his boots. The man beside the Corolla straightened up and walked on, although he could not possibly have heard him.

Pushing the car door shut, Wisting looped the radio strap across his chest. He moved towards the road through the shadows, approaching from an angle, ensuring that he would remain invisible to the other man as he crossed the street.

The suspect had left footprints in the snow on the pavement. As Wisting passed the green Corolla, he realised that the man must have turned into the car park outside the chemicals factory.

He would have preferred to be equipped with earplugs, like the guys in the Security Service. Eivind Larsen would have been able to give him directions from the car. He was reluctant to switch on the police radio, in case a sudden message warned the man ahead.

Wisting stopped where the tracks veered into the car park. Instead of following the footprints, he waded through the snow, beside a clump of bushes, and found a position affording him a good view.

It took a while before he saw the man again, hunched between two parked cars. Then he heard a click, an almost inaudible sound, and the interior light in one lit as the door opened.

Wisting took a few strides through the deep snow, sinking up to his knees, but finally managing to totter on to the car park, where he picked up his pace. The man was sitting in the driver's seat, his head dipped to one side as he fumbled to connect the leads along the steering column to get the car started.

Behind him, Eivind Larsen switched on the patrol car headlights and rolled the vehicle towards him.

With a single swift movement, the car thief raised his head and looked around. He caught sight of Wisting and flung himself out of the car.

It was the man with the pale complexion he had spotted

when they had been interrupted by the report of the bank raid in Stavern.

'Stop!' he shouted.

The man's start was barely twenty metres. Wisting was rapidly catching him when he changed direction and disappeared between two buildings. A wire fence blocked the end of the alley, but he ran straight at it, gained a foothold and jumped over.

Wisting hesitated for a moment, enough to lose both speed and power, and had to retrace his steps and take another run before he could climb the fence.

They were near Alfred Andersen's mechanical workshop. A floodlight high on the building was the only source of light.

The suspect was gone, but had left his tracks in the snow. Wisting turned on his police radio and directed Eivind Larsen to the other side of the building.

The tracks showed that the man he had been pursuing had tried the door of the workshop building before scrambling onwards. His footprints continued round a workman's shed, behind a container and towards a warehouse building in the part of the premises that was shrouded in darkness.

The warehouse had a roof, but no walls. The snow had blown in at the sides but, a couple of metres beneath the roof, the concrete floor remained clear of snow. He could follow. Snow from the grooves on the soles of the man's boots had left stains between shelves which were stacked with iron pipes and metal sheets of various thicknesses and lengths.

Suddenly the man appeared directly in front of him, aiming a kick that caught Wisting in the groin. He doubled up, groaning, and took a punch in the head. He blocked the next blow and reached for his baton.

The man pulled an iron pipe from a nearby pile and struck out, missing as Wisting jumped back. When he raised the pipe again, Wisting threw himself forward and used his shoulder to knock him off balance. Lifting his baton he struck at his opponent's upper arm, forcing him to drop his weapon. He swung the baton and struck again, this time hitting the large muscle group in the man's thigh. He yelled in pain and fell to his knees. Wisting struck his other arm before grabbing it and pulling it behind his back until he finally lay face down on the ground. Wisting sat astride him, hauled up his other arm and handcuffed them together.

Boots trudged towards him and the light from a torch danced before his eyes.

He called to Eivind Larsen and let him catch his breath before they hoisted the man to his feet and searched his pockets. He was carrying a pocketknife, a lighter and a bunch of keys.

'What's your name?' Wisting asked.

The man did not answer.

'I know him,' Larsen said. 'It's Simon Becker. I've arrested him before. I know his father as well.'

Becker was a name Wisting had seen in reports. This was the man who had been suspected of the car thefts all along.

'Okay,' he said. 'You're coming with us.'

They dragged Simon Becker with them to the patrol car and drove him to the cells at the police station.

Once Becker was installed in Cell Eight, Eivind Larsen drove out again to pick up the rucksack left behind in the stolen car and talk to the night shift workers at the chemical factory. Wisting made his way to the workroom to write a report of the arrest and draw up a charge sheet for attempted car theft. Thereafter he enclosed the papers in a green document folder and dropped them in the CID mailbox.

Next morning a few of the investigators would visit Simon Becker's apartment to conduct a search. They would then bring him up for interview. Wisting imagined the questions the interviewer would begin with and how, little by little, Becker would be confronted with the evidence. His impatience for real investigative work brought a frisson of excitement.

Two hours were left of his shift. They were called to check

a vandalised phone kiosk at Lilletorvet, and a car hit by a snowplough, before their shift was over.

Wisting dashed home to exchange a few words with Ingrid and tell her about the car thief before taking a nap. In a few hours he would meet Jan Bergan and his mother. Maybe they could provide him with the solution to the mystery of the vintage car in the barn.

15

Wisting grabbed four hours sleep before leaving, driving though Larvik and out on to the E18 in the direction of Oslo. As he joined the road an oncoming snowplough with rattling chains stirred up a white cloud. Snow piled onto the windscreen, and he dropped his speed just enough to see the road ahead. Traffic was moving at a snail's pace.

After the new tunnel at Holmestrand, he got stuck in a queue behind a lorry. He thought he had allowed plenty of time, but now wondered whether he would be late. As he drummed his fingers on the steering wheel, the microfilm at the library came to mind. If this trip yielded the result he was hoping for, he would be spared reading through reams of old newspapers.

At Sande the crawling lorry turned off the motorway, but only when the road opened into two lanes after the toll station at Drammen was he able to pick up speed. Approaching Oslo, he took the Store Ringvei bypass to avoid heavy traffic in the city centre. At Bjerke racing track he pulled into a layby and looked up his road atlas to take his bearings. Still though, he got lost twice before finding his way to the low-rise apartment block where Ragna Bergan lived on the second floor.

Her son opened the door. In his early sixties, he was tall with thick, dark hair and a beard of the same colour. They shook hands and Wisting thanked him for their phone conversation the previous day.

The apartment faced west with a view towards Oslo Fjord and the rest of the city. The coffee table was set with a porcelain coffee set and a crocheted tablecloth. Ragna Bergan came in from the kitchen with a cake dish. She had completely white hair, a stooped back and walked with a slightly shuffling gait.

Setting down the dish, she wiped her arthritic hands on her apron before shaking hands with Wisting.

'Thanks for agreeing to see me,' he said.

'Have a seat. I'll fetch the coffee.'

He sat on the settee. In the centre of the table, a framed photograph of a tall, sharp-nosed man was displayed. He was dressed in a dark chauffeur's uniform with shiny buttons and a peaked cap, and he presumed this was her late husband, Martinius Bergan. Behind him in the photo was a sleek, black, newly polished car.

'That's Dad,' Jan Bergan confirmed with a nod of his head. 'After the bankruptcy he began to drive taxis and, after the war, bought his own car. A Chevrolet.'

Jan Bergan talked as though Wisting was familiar with aspects of the Bergan family history. He was not aware of any bankruptcy, but assumed this was something that happened after the disappearance of one of the company vehicles.

Ragna Bergan, who had returned with the coffee pot, filled the three cups on the table before she sat down.

'I don't know anything about the case from 1925,' Wisting began, making sure to speak loudly and clearly. 'To the best of my knowledge, it was never investigated in my police district, but now the car has been found in our neck of the woods.'

They waited for him to continue.

'It happened by sheer chance,' he continued, explaining how Rupert Hansson was on the lookout for a classic car restoration project.

Jan Bergan enquired about specific details: who owned the barn, how the car could have been there for so long without anyone asking any questions, and what condition it was in.

Wisting answered as best he could, but refrained from mentioning the bullet holes. Nor did he say anything about how the trail of the night safe robbers had, by some fluke, ended outside the old barn.

'Did you find anything inside the car?' Jan Bergan asked.

'An old newspaper. A copy of *Aftenposten* from Monday 17 August 1925.'

'But nothing that could tell you how the car found its way there?'

'I probably know less than you do. Can you tell me what took place when the car disappeared?'

Jan Bergan glanced across at his mother. The old woman shifted in her seat.

'Martinius started the transport company with his brother in 1922,' she said. 'Their father had run a horse and cart business. When the boys were brought in, they invested in motor cars. For a long time they were the only ones who did, and they had a lot of work on their hands. They drove all over Oslo. At their peak, they had three cars and four lorries, and ten employees.'

Ragna Bergan fell silent, thinking back to a bygone era. Wisting rattled the saucer as he replaced his coffee cup, rousing her from her reverie.

'Then there was this trip to the south of Norway in 1925,' she sighed. 'Everything was kept secret. I knew nothing about it until after the consignment vanished.'

'A secret consignment?'

Ragna Bergan glanced at her son. She seemed tired and worn out, and there was a pleading in her eyes. The son took over.

'It was an assignment for Norges Bank,' Jan Bergan said. 'The company was hired to transport cash from the branch in Kristiansand to the head office in Oslo.'

'Jan was only three years old at that time,' Ragna Bergan said.

'The money was usually transported by train, but the railway workers were on strike. It was important to the bank that the consignment be transported as normal, and so Dad was given the job.'

Ragna Bergan pushed the cake dish across to Wisting and brushed crumbs from the table.

'It was strike breaking,' she said. 'That's why it all had to be kept secret. No one was to know about that trip. Not even afterwards. It was all hushed up.'

'It was vital that Norges Bank collect the money,' Jan Bergan said. 'A lot of notes were in circulation in the districts, but there was a shortage in the capital. They were about to run out. The alternative was to print more banknotes, but that would cause inflation.'

Wisting, having taken out his notebook, was scribbling down keywords. 'What happened then?'

Ragna Bergan clasped her hands on her lap. 'Marvin was the one who was driving. Martinius's brother. He never came back.'

'Car, money and driver all disappeared?'

Ragna Bergan nodded. 'At first they thought there had been an accident. The arrangement was that the money should be delivered on Thursday afternoon. When he didn't turn up, we thought he might have had a puncture or something, and been delayed. In those days it wasn't the same as now, with a phone in nearly every house. He couldn't just call and tell us he'd been delayed. As time dragged on, we thought something more serious must have happened, that he had driven off the road somewhere. On Saturday morning, Martinius sent one of the drivers to look for him, but it was useless.'

'What about the police?'

'They were brought in on the Friday, but they blamed Marvin.'

'How's that?'

'They thought he had run off with the money and Martinius and the company were held responsible. According to the contract, they were liable for reinstatement of the consignment. It was more than they were able to pay, and the company went belly-up.'

'Marvin would never have placed Dad in a situation like that,' Jan Bergan added.

His mother agreed. 'The police thought they would find

Marvin sooner or later, and that he would turn up when the money ran out. We never saw him again.'

'How much money are we talking about?'

This time it was the son who answered: 'Four hundred and fifty thousand kroner, a lot of money at that time. Nowadays it would be more than five million.'

Wisting did some mental calculations: more than thirty years' wages.

'In addition, there were five kilos of gold,' Jan Bergan continued. 'The price of gold wasn't as high as it is now. Its value has multiplied many times over.'

'Was he driving on his own, with such large sums on board?'

'The money was in a locked chest,' the old woman said. 'It was no different from being sent by train.'

'What do you believe happened?'

'Martinius thought there must have been a highway robbery.'

'What did the police say to that?'

'I don't know, but they probably didn't believe it. There were no highway robbers in Norway by that time.'

'Nobody knew about the consignment,' Jan Bergan said. 'Everything was secret, you see, because of the strike.'

'That's why Martinius thought someone from the bank in Kristiansand must have been behind it, ' his mother said. 'He thought that someone had followed Marvin and forced him off the road.'

'They would most likely have struck earlier,' Wisting said. 'Larvik is approximately halfway between Kristiansand and Oslo. That's a long way for anyone on his tail.'

The old woman tilted her head, as if he had brought something to her mind. 'Have you spoken to Ruth and Dagfinn?'

'Dagfinn's dead, Mum.'

The woman nodded and apologized. 'But what about Ruth?'

'Who are Ruth and Dagfinn?'

'Ruth is a cousin of Martinius and Marvin,' she said quietly. 'She was married to Dagfinn from Larvik. They lived down there. Marvin stopped and spent the night before he drove on to Kristiansand.'

Wisting leaned forward and jotted the names in his notebook. 'He stopped *en route*?'

'It took more than twenty hours to drive to Kristiansand at that time. He spent the night with Ruth and Dagfinn in Larvik, but also called at a couple of other places to drop off goods. In Kristiansand, he spent the night in a hotel.'

'Did the police talk to Ruth and Dagfinn at that time?'

'Several times,' she said.

'Did you talk to the police?'

'Yes, of course, but it was Martinius they wanted to speak to.'

'Do you remember the names of any of the investigators?'

'The one in charge was called Michalsen,' was her swift reply, 'and there was a young detective who went down to Larvik as well. He had a Swedish name: Gustafsson. He sounded Swedish too, a few words here and there. He lived at Skillebekk, not far from where Martinius had his garage.'

'Do you know if he's still alive?'

Ragna Bergan shook her head. 'Martinius told me he had driven him once in his taxi.' She fixed her gaze on the framed picture on the table. 'That must have been some time in the early fifties. He was only a few years older than Martinius and me.'

Wisting stared down at his notebook. He had underlined the name *Ruth*. Underlining it yet again, he asked for her surname and added: Skaugen. Ruth Skaugen.

They sat for another half hour, but nothing of consequence emerged.

'One more thing,' Wisting said, getting to his feet. 'Legally, does the car still belong to you?'

Ragna Bergan and her son exchanged glances. This thought had probably not struck them before.

'Would you consider selling it?'

'We don't want it,' Jan Bergan answered. 'I think I'd like to see it though, wherever it is now.'

His mother rose from the settee and escorted Wisting to the door with her son.

When he left, he felt he had lifted some of the burden they had been carrying and taken it upon himself. He had been unable to give them answers about what happened nearly sixty years before and, in all likelihood, had stirred up bad memories, but perhaps their minds would be easier in the knowledge that he had assumed that heavy load.

16

Wisting clambered into his car, turned the ignition and left the engine idling while he swept the windows clear of snow. Inside again, he headed for the Ringvei motorway.

After a few hundred metres, he stopped to fill up with petrol. As a woman emerged from a phone kiosk, he followed her with his eye while he filled the tank. She wrapped a scarf around her neck and set off towards one of the nearby apartment blocks.

After he had paid in the service station, he entered the phone kiosk, picked up the telephone directory and leafed through it to 'Arne Vikene'. There were two of them, but one had his title listed in smaller letters beneath his name: *Police Officer*.

Arne Viken responded at once, dismissing Wisting's apologies for calling him at home.

'Thanks for your fax,' Wisting went on, saying that he had spoken to the widow of the man who owned the veteran car.

'Is she willing to sell the car?'

'Yes, but I'm afraid I already have a buyer.'

'That's okay. It'll be splendid to see it back on the road.'

'There was another thing I was wondering. You've worked in the Oslo police for a long time. Do you know an investigator called Gustafsson who lived in Skillebekk?'

'The Swede, yes. I worked with him in the sixties. He's retired now. Has been for years, but drops into the police station for pensioner meetings. What do you want with him?'

'There were some unusual circumstances surrounding the disappearance of the car. They suspected a company employee of misappropriating both the car and its cargo. Gustafsson investigated the case.'

'Aha, I see. He was widowed before he retired from the force. I think he still lives in Skillebekk, though. Ragnar Gustafsson. If you don't get hold of him, I can track him down through the personnel office.'

Wisting thanked Arne Viken for his assistance and thumbed through the phone book to find Ragnar Gustafsson. He inserted another couple of coins and dialled the number. He was on the verge of hanging up when a hoarse voice answered: 'Yes, hello?'

'Am I speaking to Ragnar Gustafsson?'

'Who's asking?'

Wisting explained who he was and that he worked for the Larvik police. 'It's about a cash consignment transported by Kristiania Haulage Company that disappeared in 1925. Do you remember the case?'

'Yes, what about it?'

'I've found the car.'

Gustafsson's breathing grew more laboured. 'Where?'

'Hidden in a barn. I have a witness statement to the effect that it was wheeled in one summer's night in 1925. It's been there ever since.'

'And the driver?'

A tractor had started to clear the snow from the parking area in front of the phone box. Wisting raised his voice.

'I've no information about him. Neither him nor the money, but everything points to an ambush. There are two bullet holes in the car.'

'That just deepens the mystery,' Gustafsson said.

A coin dropped into the prepayment box. 'I'm in Oslo just now. Could I meet you?'

'Gabels gate 9B. Ground floor.'

Expressing his thanks, Wisting wound up the conversation and got back into his car. He found the address in the road atlas and manoeuvred his way towards the city centre. Half an hour later, he was seated in front of a huge tiled Swedish stove in Ragnar Gustafsson's dining room.

The former detective had become an old man, with hollow cheeks and liver spots on his hands. His eyes had taken on a milky haze.

Wisting explained how chance circumstances had led to the car being found.

'It had to happen sooner or later.' Ragnar Gustafsson clenched the fist that was resting on the table. Loose skin tightened across his knuckles.

'You investigated the case. Did the police have a theory about what happened?'

Gustafsson opened and closed his hand as he thought.

'The police inspector's conclusion was that the driver had run off with both the car and the money. Strictly speaking, there were no grounds for believing anything else. You see, there was a railway dispute. All transport to and from Oslo was affected. The bank authorities were dependent on the supply of banknotes from the regions to ensure enough notes in circulation. That was why it was decided to convey the cash by car.'

Wisting already knew this, but let the old man talk. It might help with the recall of details.

'We weren't dealing with a regular consignment that anyone could plan to ambush. On the contrary, really. The job could be regarded as strike breaking, and so it was carried out in secrecy. There were only a few people who knew. The brother, whom the driver ran the transport company with, the managers at the bank in Oslo and a few trusted employees in Kristiansand. If anyone had the idea of enriching himself through it, it had to be someone on the inside. The most obvious person was the driver who had a case containing several hundred thousand kroner on the back seat of his car. It was easy to arrive at the conclusion that the temptation became too great.'

'The bullet holes suggest an ambush,' said Wisting. 'The location and direction of the shots point to the driver being hit.'

Ragnar Gustafsson placed one hand over the other and rubbed them together. 'His name was Marvin. It is comingback to me. The driver's name was Marvin Bergan. He ran the transport company with his brother.'

Wisting took out his notebook and told him that he had paid a visit to the widow of that brother, Martinius Bergan.

'She told me that the driver made a few stops on the trip down. Could anyone have worked out where he was going and what he was doing, and then lain in wait for him on the way back?'

'That's a possibility.' Gustafsson bit his lower lip and stared at a point on the wall. Almost a minute ticked past. Wisting was reluctant to break the silence.

'Now it's coming back.' Gustafsson tapped his forehead with his finger. 'The cogs turn slowly these days, I'm afraid, but I remember that he delivered machine parts to the iron foundry in Drammen and some documents to the landowner at Bærums Verk. I talked to both the landowner and the foreman at the iron foundry, but what turned out to be of interest was the time he had spent down in your stamping ground in Larvik.'

A light appeared in Gustafsson's weary eyes. It was as if he was making fresh discoveries in his memory.

'He had an overnight stay with a family on his way to the south coast. He had intended to stop there on the way back too, but that didn't happen.'

'With Ruth and Dagfinn Skaugen?'

Ragnar Gustafsson pointed his forefinger at Wisting and jabbed it in the air to emphasise that these were the right names. 'I went down there to talk to them. A few of the relatives were gathered. Some neighbours and workers were there too. I interviewed them all over three days.'

'What did you learn?'

'Nothing. Marvin Bergan arrived in the afternoon. It was a hot summer's day. They had sat in the garden until late evening. Bergan had been given the use of a bedroom belonging to one of the children in the house. He drove on the next morning. He said that he was to pick up a consignment in Kristiansand, but didn't mention what it was.'

Leaning back, Wisting tried to envisage the people gathered around the table in the garden on that warm summer evening in 1925. Could Marvin Bergan have let slip to anyone what sort of mission he was on?

'Do you know where the case notes are kept today?'

Ragnar Gustafsson pulled a face, as if this was a difficult question. 'We packed up all the papers after six months. I haven't seen them since then. They were stored in the basement at the police station in Victoria terrasse. Then the war came, and in the fifties most of them disappeared when the archives were destroyed in a fire. If you're lucky, it could be that the case files were transferred to the State Archives before that. You won't find any answers in those old papers. They only contain all the blind alleys.'

'What would you have done,' Wisting asked, 'if you were to take up the investigation again?'

Another gleam appeared in the old man's misty eyes.

'I would retrace the route he took, and check every single person he met on the way to Kristiansand. Four hundred and fifty thousand kroner vanished into thin air that day. That's a lot of money. Money that must have left traces in a person's life, either for good or ill.'

17

Wisting arrived home an hour before he was due on night shift. The twins were asleep, and Ingrid sat reading a book. He gave her a kiss before going through to see Thomas and Line. A really special atmosphere filled a room where two children slept. Their breathing was regular, and their faces peaceful and calm.

When he returned to the living room, Ingrid laid her book aside and he told her what he had discovered.

'What are you going to do now?' she asked.

'I'll have to write a report about my findings, and hand it to Ove Dokken.'

'What will happen after that?'

'That'll be up to him, but they're so busy with the night safe robbery that it'll probably be put aside. The case has been in abeyance for almost sixty years. It won't do any harm to let it lie for a while longer.'

Before he headed back to work, he drank two cups of coffee in the forlorn hope that they would pick him up. At the station, he only ever managed half a cup before driving out on patrol. Friday nights were always hectic with a lot of restaurant disturbances, especially now during the Christmas party season. Not until after three were they able to drive back to the police station, having dealt with a fight in a taxi queue.

He carried a cup of coffee into the Criminal Investigation Department. Ove Dokken's office door was open, as usual, and the case files for the past week were lying on his desk. Wisting stood in semi-darkness and leafed through them until he located the folder marked 'Simon Becker'.

The man they had arrested had appeared in court and been remanded in custody.

He flicked through the papers to the interview statement. Within the first few paragraphs Simon Becker confessed to the attempted car theft and assault of the police officer who had arrested him.

This was a common strategy of habitual criminals, confessing to crimes impossible to escape. Often the police would content themselves with what was handed to them on a plate, and the suspect would avoid further scrutiny.

However, Simon Becker had not evaded such attention. In the next paragraph, he was confronted with two car stereos found under the bed at his home. He claimed he had bought them from a man whose name he did not know.

Questions were also asked about a pair of sunglasses, a white college sweater carrying the Ball logo in pink letters, and music cassettes picked up in his apartment: David Bowie's *Let's Dance*, *Thriller* by Michael Jackson, and *Sunday People* by The Monroes. Simon Becker explained that he had bought these in various service stations, and that he had owned the sunglasses for a long time. He said the same about the sweater.

Towards the end of the interview, he was asked about a black Sierra, stolen a fortnight earlier. He denied having anything to do with it.

Wisting browsed through the case notes to a report that referred to another case. One of the investigators had taken an additional statement from the man whose stolen car had been used in the bank raid. He had described items left in the vehicle, including a white Ball sweater, a pair of Ray-Ban sunglasses and a number of cassettes, including the latest albums by David Bowie, Michael Jackson and The Monroes.

Wisting smiled with satisfaction. The report confirmed his suspicions. Simon Becker had stolen the car used in the robbery. Wisting thought he had probably not been involved in the robbery itself. He would be most unlikely to go out only a few nights later to steal another car. More probably he had emptied it of valuables before getting rid of it, but it meant that the robbery had a local connection.

He flipped through to the report dealing with the confiscated items. In addition to the two car stereos and items from the Sierra, notebooks, diaries, loose memos and papers had been seized. Wisting followed the investigators' line of thinking. They had been looking for a link between Simon Becker and the person to whom he had delivered the stolen Sierra, a tie-up with the robbers.

The evidence store was situated farther along the corridor, but protocols had been tightened after Wrangsund had been caught stealing. The key now had to be signed for through the Chief Inspector, but the main key was kept down at the duty desk.

He descended the stairs to his own section, where Haugen and Storvolden were sleeping in their armchairs in the staff-room. Crossing the room to the Duty Sergeant's desk, he pulled out the drawer where the key was kept, and took it with him.

The evidence store had no windows, so he turned on the ceiling light. The Simon Becker items were on one of the near-est shelves: the music cassettes, sunglasses, sweater, stereo equipment and a cardboard box containing various papers. These were little notes with only a phone number or sum of money scribbled on them, sometimes accompanied by initials or a date. It would take time to sort through these, with no guarantee of anything to take the investigators forward.

He studied a small notebook filled with phone numbers, different forenames and nicknames. Mostly they were local numbers, but there was a sprinkling for Sandefjord and Tønsberg. No Oslo numbers. He reflected for a few minutes, and decided to take a photocopy to check whether he could find any names from previous cases in which Simon Becker had been found guilty.

He brought the notebook through to the photocopy room and switched on the machine. It took a while to heat up. While he waited, his portable radio crackled.

'Wisting to the duty room!'

He lifted the radio and gave a response.

'Report of house fire in Byskogen,' Storvolden said.

'Received.'

The photocopier was ready. He pressed the big green button and heard the machine labour slowly underneath the lid, finally dropping a photocopied sheet into the tray at the side.

Although the copy was difficult to read, it would have to do. He turned off the machine and returned the notebook to the evidence store before dashing downstairs.

'Haugen's waiting in the car,' Storvolden said from his desk. 'Where the hell have you been?'

'In the loo,' Wisting answered, tossing the key back in the drawer. Storvolden gave him a quizzical look as he rushed out to the waiting car.

The house was in flames when they arrived, and enormous sheets of sparks swirled into the night sky. The fire service was already on the scene, but were having difficulty with their equipment. The house owner stood in the snow with a blanket around his shoulders and a pair of green Wellington boots on his feet. Wisting approached.

The entire family had managed to escape, he explained, nodding at his neighbour's kitchen window where four faces watched the fire.

Wisting updated Storvolden by radio and faced the man again, conscious of how difficult it was to acknowledge another person's despair while behaving professionally.

'Do you know how the fire started?'

It transpired that the man had been redecorating the living room, and thought that was where the fire had started. It was possible that oily rags had burst into flames.

At last the fire crew managed to get their hoses going. Wisting stood with the householder until the man had seen enough and withdrew into the neighbour's house.

When he left the scene a few hours later, nothing but a smoking ruin was left.

The night shift was nearing its end. Before he went home he sat at a typewriter and produced a report. In a matter of months, all thought of the incident would be gone. In a few years' time, he would probably have experienced so much else that he would struggle to remember the fire at all. For the people affected, however, the recollections would be scorched into their memories and remain there for the rest of their lives.

In the street outside the police station, a snowplough rumbled past. Wisting stood up, wondering what Ruth Skaugen would be able to recall from the summer of 1925.

18

Monday morning found Wisting on a wooden chair in the corridor outside Chief Inspector Ove Dokken's office. On his lap was a report of everything he knew about the vintage car in the barn at Tveidalen and the cash consignment in 1925.

Off duty at the weekend, he had stayed at home with Ingrid and the twins, but had gone over the wording in his head repeatedly. On Sunday afternoon, they had visited his parents-in-law and he had borrowed an old typewriter from Ingrid's father to fill in a blank report form he had brought home.

One of the women from the records office offered him coffee in a paper cup while he waited. He knew her, but could not for the life of him remember her name.

'They usually keep going until quarter to nine,' she said, with a nod in the direction of Dokken's office door. He thanked her.

At ten to nine the door opened and the section leaders came out, leaving Dokken sitting alone behind a stack of case papers. Grabbing a packet of cigarettes, he coaxed one out.

Wisting popped his head round the door. 'Do you have a minute?'

'Is this about the robbery again?' Dokken asked, lighting his cigarette.

'No, it's another case. An old case.'

The Chief Inspector inhaled. 'It's Monday morning, Wisting,' he sighed, letting smoke ooze through his nostrils. 'It's a bad day and a bad time to raise the subject of old cases.' He laid his hand on the pile of documents on his desk. 'I've more than enough on my plate.'

'I can come back tomorrow, then.'

'Sit down!' Dokken growled, glancing at the clock. 'You've got five minutes before I have to go to a meeting about the night safe raid.'

Wisting sat down smartly. 'I've written a report,' he said, putting down the papers.

Dokken let them lie.

'It's to do with a consignment of cash that disappeared nearly sixty years ago. I think I might have stumbled on something.'

Dokken sat back to listen, without asking any questions or interrupting until Wisting had said all he had to say.

'Are you on duty just now?'

'No, I just came in to deliver the report.'

Stubbing out his cigarette, Dokken took another look at the time. 'Do you have a plan?' he asked.

'What do you mean?'

'I hope you haven't come to unload all this on to me without any suggestion as to what should be done. What would you do, if you were a detective?'

'I would try to locate the old case files. I would remove the car, examine the barn and conduct another interview with Ruth Skaugen.'

Dokken rose from his chair. 'Do that. I can give you twenty hours' overtime.'

Wisting stared at him.

'Do you mean I should work on the case, as the investigator?'

Dokken picked up a sheaf of papers and headed for the door. 'Start with Ruth Skaugen, and keep me posted.'

Wisting got to his feet and made his way to the empty office he had borrowed a few days earlier. He would have to tell Ingrid he would not be home anytime soon.

19

Ruth Skaugen lived in Brekke. Wisting phoned ahead to find that Jan Bergan had already called. She gave Wisting directions and agreed to meet him at eleven o'clock.

He used his own car but took a portable police radio. After he had left the main road and driven some distance through a snowy white landscape of rolling fields, he came to a group of houses surrounded by tall pine trees. These were the buildings attached to Brekke farm.

The farmyard had been cleared of snow. He parked, picked up the radio and stepped out.

Ruth Skaugen was waiting at the door by the time he reached the steps. She had silver grey hair, glasses and a network of wrinkles on her face. She used a walking stick for support as she ushered him into the kitchen where a stove was lit. Coffee cups were ready on the table, together with a jug of cream and a plate of buttered *lefse*. He sat while the old woman lifted the coffee pot from the hotplate and poured.

'You've found the car at last?' She took a seat by the window.

'Not very far from here.' He went on to tell her about the barn in Tveidalen.

'But no sign of Marvin?'

'I'd hoped you could tell me about the last time you saw him. Do you remember that evening?'

'Of course,' she said. 'It was the last time we saw him. What's more, we had to talk to the police about it, time after time afterwards.'

Wisting waited for her to go on.

'Really there's not much to tell,' she said.

'Yes, but all the same...' Wisting took out his notebook.

'He arrived here without warning,' she began. 'That wasn't so good. He had received short notice himself, you see, and we didn't have a telephone in those days.'

She gazed through the window to the road. 'He turned up just before dinner time. Fortunately, I had made a big pot of chicken stew. It was so hot that summer we were sitting outside. He'd been thinking of staying overnight at the Hotel Wassilioff, which had just been rebuilt after the fire. Of course, we wouldn't allow that and insisted he stay here. I made up a bed in Guttorm's room. He's our youngest son, and he slept with us that night.'

'Who was here that evening, apart from you and your husband?'

'Dagfinn's brother was here all day with Johannes from the farm on the other side of Furubrekka.' She pointed out the window to the west. 'There was a hired man as well. They were working on the construction of the new hay barn.'

Wisting leaned across the table. 'Who was the hired man?'

Ruth Skaugen raised her cup to her mouth. 'I can't remember now,' she answered, taking a sip. 'He was a man Johannes had got hold of. Dagfinn wasn't entirely happy with him. The work was progressing slowly, and he was slipshod. You should find his name in the old papers. The Oslo police were here and spoke to him too.'

'What about Johannes? Is he still alive?'

She shook her head as she pushed the plate across the table to him. 'You have to taste the *lefse*,' she insisted. 'My daughter made them. I've stopped baking nowadays.'

Wisting helped himself as he glanced at his notes. 'What was his full name?'

'Johannes Brekka,' the old woman replied, and she too helped herself to one of the *lefse*.

'What about Dagfinn's brother, what was his name?'

'Kai. Kai Skaugen.'

Wisting jotted this down.

'After dinner Hans cycled over to see us. He brought some strawberries and cream.'

'Hans?' Wisting asked.

'Hans Ole Manvik.'

'So, the people who were here, apart from you and Dagfinn, were your brother-in-law, Kai Skaugen, your neighbour Johannes Brekka, Hans Ole Manvik, and a hired workman.'

'And Johannes's eldest son, Karstein.' She rose abruptly. 'I've got a photograph. Karstein was an apprentice photographer at Ludwigsen's in town. He wanted to photograph them while they were building the barn. He stayed for dinner and took photos.'

Ruth Skaugen disappeared into the living room and returned with an album. 'Yes, and the children were here, of course.' She remembered when she had leafed to the appropriate page. 'Gunnar, Guttorm and Solveig.'

She placed the album on the table in front of Wisting. 'And Anna came for dinner too.' She returned to her seat by the window.

Wisting felt a prickling sensation in the pit of his stomach. Sixty years ago, Anna was probably one of the most common names. It was popular today as well, of course, but it was the name on the envelope he had found in the barn in Tveidalen.

'Who was Anna?'

Ruth Skaugen's mouth puckered ever so slightly. 'She's at the very back of the photograph, on the left. She was Kai's fiancée. They married subsequently, but I don't have any contact with her these days. Kai is dead.'

Wisting studied the old picture. Slightly discoloured, it showed signs of age, but for anyone who knew the people, it would be possible to recognise faces. Seven adults and three children, all gathered around a table in the garden with the old Minerva standing in a corner in the background.

'Is that Marvin Bergan?' he asked, pointing at a young man in a white, short-sleeved shirt.

Ruth Skaugen leaned across the table. 'Yes,' she said, and pointed out the others.

He studied them all. The woman called Anna was standing beside her future husband, Kai. Ruth was wearing an apron and a headscarf. He could see that she was a hard-working woman: pale and thin, her face looked drawn. Anna was different. Her dark hair hung in loose curls on her shoulders and she smiled warmly at the photographer.

'Why don't you have any contact with Anna?'

Ruth Skaugen chewed on a piece of *lefse* for a long time.

'Dagfinn had three brothers,' she said. 'They were all very different, but Kai was perhaps the one who stood out most. He didn't have a regular job, and that's why Dagfinn had him working here for a while. He didn't want to go to sea either.'

'And he married Anna?'

'They had two daughters, but I don't think things went too well for them.'

'How's that?'

'I think they'd both made a poor marriage and he started to drink, just like his father.'

Wisting flicked through his notes and found the name written on the rucksack in the barn.

'Does the name Alfred Danielsen or Davidsen mean anything to you?'

Ruth Skaugen peered down at his notebook. 'Anna's name was Danielsen before she got married. I wonder whether her father's name might have been Alfred. Why do you ask?'

'It's just a name that's cropped up,' Wisting said, leafing further through his notes. 'The barn where the car was found belonged to Peder Heian. Are you familiar with that name?'

Ruth Skaugen shook her head.

He ran through his notes again, this time to the list of people present in August 1925. There were a lot of names.

'Do you recall what you talked about that evening?'

The wrinkles on the old woman's face stretched as she smiled. 'My goodness, what did we talk about ... well, the men were chatting about the new barn, and then we almost certainly talked about the weather. That was such a hot summer.'

'What about Marvin? What did he talk about?'

'He told us how things were at home. He was still living with his parents at that time.'

'Didn't he say anything about where he was going, or what kind of job he was on?'

'Yes he did, of course, he was quite proud of it.'

Wisting sat upright. The prickling sensation had returned to his stomach. Stronger this time. 'Did he tell you he was going to Kristiansand to collect money?'

She nodded. 'He was driving to Kristiansand the next day. He was going to stay overnight at a hotel and pick up the money on the Wednesday morning. That night he was going to stop here again. We joked about what he would do with the money that night.'

'So, everyone here that evening knew about the consignment of cash?'

'We didn't know how much it was,' she said. 'Marvin didn't either, just that it would be stored in a sealed metal box.'

Wisting drummed his pen on his notebook, unsure how to proceed. 'Before the weekend I met a former policeman who worked on the case and interviewed you in 1925,' he said.

Ruth Skaugen nodded. 'As you say, there was a policeman from Oslo here. Although I actually think he was Swedish.'

'Ragnar Gustafsson. He said that Marvin Bergan hadn't mentioned the money to anyone.'

Ruth Skaugen clasped her hands around her coffee cup again. 'That's right. Everything about the consignment had to be kept secret. If it got out that anyone had taken the strikers' work there would be a real fuss. Marvin and Martinius could be accused of strike breaking, but it's such a long time ago that it can't be dangerous to talk about it now. The company went bankrupt because of what happened.'

'Why didn't you tell this to the police at the time?'

It seemed Ruth Skaugen did not understand the question.

'Because it was a secret,' she answered. 'Marvin wasn't supposed to talk to anyone about it.'

It took some time before Wisting could fathom the old woman's train of thought. 'What you're saying is that you were scared Marvin had done something wrong by telling you about it, and so you refrained from telling the police.'

'We didn't want to create any problems for him, you see.'

Ruth Skaugen crossed to the stove to fetch the coffee pot while Wisting remained seated, lost in thought.

The family's misplaced loyalty had given the investigation a totally misguided starting point. The simplest character of a lie is the embellishment of truth, smoothing over your own mistakes or those of other people. Before him now was a fresh opportunity that had been denied the investigation in 1925.

Ruth Skaugen poured more coffee. Wisting waited until she had sat down again. 'Who suggested that you shouldn't say anything about what Marvin had revealed?'

'It was probably a joint decision. A joint understanding.'

'Someone must have been first to say it out loud?'

The old woman gave this some thought. 'Well ...' She shook her head. 'Dagfinn and I talked about it that evening before the Swedish policeman turned up. When we were gathered together, it seemed as if the others had come to the same conclusion.'

'What do you mean by "when we were gathered together"?'

'We were all here the day the policeman was to arrive. He was a bit late, but took each of us, one by one, into the parlour to interview us. Dagfinn went first and, when he came out, he told us that he hadn't said anything about the consignment of money. All the rest of us followed suit.'

'It was your husband's idea?'

Ruth Skaugen shook her head. 'It was more that he said he'd done what we had all already agreed.'

'But who suggested it? Who introduced the idea?'

It seemed as if the old woman did not understand the question. 'It was just something we were all agreed upon. No one disagreed.'

Wisting leaned back in his chair. 'What did you think had happened?'

She folded her thin fingers. 'At that time we probably thought Marvin had driven off the road and the car must be lying in a ditch. Now, I haven't a clue. I can't bring myself to believe what the police concluded, that he had taken the money for himself. He must have been attacked by someone who knew about it.'

'Someone here that evening Marvin stayed the night?' Wisting held up the old photograph.

The suggestion terrified her. He could see in those big eyes that this was the first time the thought had struck her.

'Could one of them have passed on the information?' he asked. 'Someone who came into a lot of money afterwards?'

Now the response came swiftly. 'No. Certainly not. On the contrary, we all struggled to make ends meet.'

'The hired man too?'

'I don't remember his name, but he did casual work on other farms later. I don't think he ever made much of himself.'

Wisting's attention returned to the list of names, and went through them one more time. The only one still alive was her sister-in-law, Anna Skaugen.

'As far as I know, she lives in town,' Ruth Skaugen said.

Wisting sat for a while longer, eating yet another of the delicious *lefse*, asking the same questions again, this time from a different angle in the hope that more details might emerge. They did not, but he had gained more from the meeting than he had dared anticipate.

This investigation depended on recreating the past, he thought, as he got into his car and drove off. Finding out who was where, as well as when and why, was a matter of asking questions and digging. Manoeuvring his way forward to people who might be in possession of answers. Obtaining fresh information and stacking it on top of what he already knew, so that a picture of what had happened became increasingly clear. He revelled in this work.

20

Anna Skaugen.

Wisting spoke the name aloud. He wanted to take the sealed envelope with him when he called on her, which meant he had to return to the barn.

Unsure whether Knut Heian had put a new padlock on the double doors, as he had promised, he drove out to Tveidal-skrysset.

Tractor tracks in the snow indicated that Heian had visited recently. Wisting followed these to the barn, where he could see the new padlock from the driving seat; bulkier than the old one, it looked more robust.

He reversed out again and found his way to the farmstead where Knut Heian was examining the blades on the snow-plough. He pulled off his work gloves and shook Wisting's hand in welcome.

'Have you found out any more about the car?' he asked.

Wisting drew his lapels together at the neck as wet, heavy snow buffeted his face. 'I've tracked down the owner's descend-ants.'

'Are they willing to sell?' Heian asked. 'If not, I thought I should really charge them rent for storage.'

'I think it will sort itself out, but a couple of things have cropped up. The car is registered as misappropriated.'

'What does that mean?'

'It originally belonged to a haulage company in Oslo, and the police concluded that one of the drivers made off with it in 1925.'

'Stolen?'

'In a way,' Wisting answered, pleased not to have to go into detail. 'The driver's name was Marvin Bergan. He was related to Ruth and Dagfinn Skaugen who live here in Larvik. Do those names mean anything to you?'

Knut Heian shook his head emphatically. 'Skaugen is a name I've heard, of course, but I don't know of any connection.'

'Now that the car has been found, it's become a police matter again. There are a couple of things I need to investigate inside the barn. Is that okay with you?'

Heian glanced at the tractor. 'Can you see to it on your own?'

Wisting nodded and Heian made for the farmhouse. 'You'll need to take the key for the new padlock with you,' he said. He returned with a key attached to a label marked *BARN* in capital letters.

'I'll bring it back in an hour or so,' Wisting promised.

'Just drop it in the mailbox if I'm out.'

Wisting drove back but was held up behind a lorry with slushy snow whirling in its wake. It sped onwards through the treacherous conditions when Wisting turned off at Tveidalskrysset.

When he picked up his police radio and a flashlight, it crossed his mind that he should really have brought a camera too. He would have to come back later with a crime scene technician to document his findings.

It occurred to him that a camera would be an excellent Christmas present for Ingrid. They already had one, but she complained about picture quality and that the flash did not function properly. It would be an expensive gift, but the money would come from the twenty hours of overtime Dokken had allocated him. Anyway, it was something they needed. It would be lovely to have good pictures of the children from the time when they were little. He would buy two photo albums, and wrap them up to present to each of the twins as a Christmas gift.

Snow had accumulated again in front of the barn doors. He cleared it away with his boots, smiling all the while and feeling pleased with his bright idea for such suitable Christmas gifts.

The key turned easily in the new padlock and he opened the doors as far as possible to let in the maximum amount of daylight.

Snow that had had fallen through holes in the roof or blown in through gaps in the walls lay in patches here and there.

He picked his way to the makeshift bed, where he located the old rucksack and extracted the letter.

He considered reading it, but felt a sense of respect for other people's mail. He also thought he recalled, from his hours spent studying criminal law, that opening other people's letters was punishable by up to two years' imprisonment; also, the police needed a court order to do so in the course of an investigation.

Putting the letter inside his jacket pocket, he checked the name on the rucksack once more. It most resembled Danielsen. Alfred Danielsen was Anna's father. It probably meant that he was the one who had written the letter and slept like a down-and-out in the barn in 1973.

He peered at the old car, still hidden beneath the tarpaulin, but could not make any connection between the events of 1925 and those of 1973. Anna and her husband Kai knew about the consignment of money. Was it mere coincidence that her father, almost fifty years later, had holed up in the same place where the car was hidden? Or did he play some part in the story?

He moved the flashlight beam around, stopping at the ladder on the opposite side. He still had not shaken off the idea that whoever had been staying in the barn was still somewhere inside. He was not entirely sure what gave him that feeling; some kind of intuition that told him the letter was a farewell missive and the remains of whoever had written it were here among the junk.

Old men hang themselves or shoot themselves. That was

what sprang to his mind. In his brief police career, he had already cut down a man who had hanged himself in the stair well between two floors while the rest of the family lay asleep. Another had shot himself in the head with a shotgun. As a trainee, he had assisted in resuscitation efforts on a woman who had taken an overdose and fallen asleep in the bathtub.

He aimed the flashlight at the beams high on the ceiling, with ropes and chains hanging from them. It would be easy to hang yourself if you did not have access to a gun. Suicide by gunshot would be quicker and less painful but, if he had used a gun, he must have hidden it somewhere. It was not logical, but people who had decided to commit suicide seldom thought in a rational fashion.

Somewhere above his head the old wooden beams creaked, and snow drizzled from one of the holes in the roof.

There was only one way to find out for certain. He put down the rucksack and placed the flashlight on an oak barrel so that it shone over the barn interior. Lifting the corrugated metal sheets, he found a wheelbarrow with no wheels and a few rolls of chicken wire. He moved these and stood in front of the empty potato crates that Knut Heian had played with as a child.

Stacked with the open ends facing him, they were like partition walls in a colossal dolls house. A little log chair was perched on one corner of the top crate, and he could see some childish drawings hanging on the walls. The opening on the bottom crate was covered. A woollen blanket was tucked beneath the crate that formed the storey above, and was suspended like a curtain to conceal whatever might be inside.

He stepped back and picked up his torch, took hold of the blanket, lifted it to one side and directed the beam of light into the crate.

Two wooden swords lay inside, as well as a bow with no string and a bundle of arrows. In the corner, old cowboy magazines: Hopalong Cassidy and Tex Willer.

He dropped the curtain again. The secret play area had

been left untouched since Knut Heian was a lad, or else other children had come across it later and played the same games.

He shone the light around the vast space inside the barn. A passageway led past parts of an old wood-burning stove and a whetstone. Farther in was a horse-drawn carriage with its collapsible hood up.

He moved an old demijohn and pushed his way forward. He used a few milk churns and a stack of margarine packing cases for support and finally brought himself level with the carriage.

Inside, on the seat, were human remains.

21

Wisting moved the flashlight from one hand to the other. Bones, with no trace of skin or flesh, lay scattered. Some were on the floor, but he had no doubt that they were from a human being. The skull, with empty eye sockets and a gaping mouth of splintered teeth, lay on the carriage seat. A few dirty rags were all that was left of the clothes.

It felt unreal. He had worked out that there must be a body somewhere in the barn, but nevertheless was astonished. At the same time, he felt a certain satisfaction that his suspicions had been confirmed. His gut feeling was something worth listening to.

The sight filled him with a sense of solemnity, as he had experienced several times before, whenever he came close to other people's sorrow, despair, or death.

He put one foot on the running board and hoisted himself to a better vantage point. It took a while for him to find what he was looking for. Between scraps of fabric and pale bones on the floor, the muzzle of a gun protruded. A pistol. He could not see all of it, and was reluctant to touch anything, but he thought it looked like a Luger. The muzzle indicated a relatively heavy calibre, perhaps nine millimetre.

A gust of wind whistled through the exterior walls and the joints of the old building creaked, like the rigging on a sailing ship in a storm.

As Wisting stood up, he leaned over the skull and used the flashlight to study it properly. It had crush injuries at the back of the head and parts of the skull itself were missing. The frayed edges around the star-shaped opening were folded outwards.

Although he was no expert, it was not difficult to envisage a chain of events. The man had sat down in the carriage, opened his mouth over the muzzle and pulled the trigger.

He aimed the light at the hood and rapidly spotted what he was after: at head height, a hole caused by the projectile's onward trajectory.

His hypothesis tallied: suicide. At least, it was difficult to deduce anything else. He had no idea how long it took for there to be nothing but a skeleton left of a body, but imagined that it had to be years. If he used the newspaper on the mattress as an indication of the date, the dead body had been here for ten years. Most of the clothes had rotted away or been eaten by rodents. What was left was a leather belt with a metal buckle and man's wristwatch. In addition, there was a pair of grey woollen socks that looked fairly well preserved. The boots were beside the mattress, probably size forty-five or forty-six, almost confirming that the skeleton belonged to a man. Experts would establish the sex by examining the bones. Maybe they would be able to say something about the age as well.

The police radio looped over his chest crackled into life: a patrol calling in that their assignment had been completed.

He speculated whether he should report his discovery over the radio, or whether he should go out, lock the door behind him and drive to the police station. Before he had reached a decision, the timbers above him made noises he did not much like. He pointed the flashlight beam at the ceiling, where the beams were buckling and tensing under the weight of snow that had fallen in recent days. A loud bang sounded as one of the beams cracked.

Splinters of wood exploded in every direction, and parts of the roof gave way with a splitting, slicing clatter. Heavy, wet snow cascaded through the hole that opened up. With a tremendous crash, half the barn roof came tumbling down and he was sent flying in a horrendous tumult of dust, roof tiles, wooden planks, and snow. The splintering noise overhead warned of more to come and, with another clap of thunder, the rest of the roof came loose.

22

Wisting checked that he was uninjured. The barn had collapsed around him, but he had managed to fling himself into one of the empty potato crates. Quick thinking had saved his life and he was now curled inside a protective little pocket. He did not know how thick the layer of snow and building materials above him might be, but it was probably just a matter of time before the packing crate caved in.

His flashlight was gone and his police radio hung by a strap, diagonally across his chest. He pressed the send button and released it again, but did not hear the usual hissing and click that would confirm contact with base. The signal out here was bad, and would have deteriorated beneath the heavy load that had buried him. Nevertheless, he tried to call the Duty Sergeant at the police station. No answer.

Struggling to find his bearings, he crawled to the side of the crate where the snow had piled up in front of the opening and sealed off the confined space. He dug his way forward, shovelling snow behind him with his hands. His fingers touched something that felt like one of the wooden swords and he pushed it into the snow, diagonally upward, and then withdrew in the hope of seeing daylight. It was too thick. Using his hand to grip the sword, he pushed his arm into the snow to extend its range. This time, when he pulled the sword back again, he could make out a glimmer of dim, grey light that gave him renewed strength.

As he dug his way upwards, he succeeded in loosening some of the clumps and wriggled forward through the passageway he had created. He forced the excavated snow backwards with

113

both hands, under his stomach. Halfway through, he took a break and tried the police radio again. Still no contact.

He scrabbled back, casting about for the wooden sword to push ahead of him as he slithered up along the snow tunnel. This time he broke right through, and a blast of fresh, cold air hit his face.

It took him another quarter of an hour to dig a hole big enough to squeeze his whole body through. He clambered out of the snow and rubble, found his footing and trudged out of the demolished barn. Wet and chilled to the bone, he gazed at a scene of devastation.

The interior wall, where the veteran car was located, was still standing. The remains of a pair of lopsided roof beams hung down, and the car itself was blanketed in snow.

He returned to his car, sat behind the steering wheel, and looked at himself in the mirror. His drenched hair was plastered to his scalp, and he was bleeding from a cut beside his left eye.

Once he had started the engine, he backed onto the main road. It had stopped snowing, he noticed. There was blue sky above the pine trees. The sun was low on the horizon and on its way down. Soon it would be dark.

23

Chief Inspector Ove Dokken was rounding off a call when Wisting entered his office, still wet and bedraggled. The telephone on the desk rang again. He lifted the receiver, but put it down when he caught sight of Wisting.

'Good grief!'

Wisting sat down. The phone started to ring again, but Dokken put the receiver to one side and lit a cigarette.

Wisting came straight to the point: 'I found a body.'

Dokken swore and shook his head in consternation, as if faced with an impossible teenager.

Wisting, about to continue, was interrupted by a section leader speaking from the door. 'We're waiting in the conference room,' he said.

Dokken looked at the clock and then back at his colleague. 'Go on without me, I'll come when I'm ready.'

'The night safe robbery,' Dokken said. 'The Oslo police are going into action tonight. We're contributing two men to the raid.'

'A breakthrough?'

'It's a gang from Tveita,' Dokken said, with a dismissive wave of his hand. 'Tell me about the body.'

Wisting told his story and Dokken listened without interrupting.

'Are you injured?'

'Nothing serious.'

The section leader returned, but did not speak. Dokken got to his feet and stubbed out his cigarette before grabbing a bundle of papers.

'This is how we'll tackle it,' he said. 'Seal off the area around the barn. I'll get hold of two men who can keep watch out there tonight, and we can dig out that skeleton of yours at first light. In the meantime, you can write a report that we'll present to the Superintendent early tomorrow.'

Wisting was happy to go along with this.

'Don't do anything else,' Dokken told him as he made for the door. 'No more interviews or anything. Hold everything in abeyance until tomorrow.'

Pausing in the doorway, he watched Wisting as he rose from his chair.

'The very first thing you need to do is get into some dry clothes,' he said. 'You can't go home to your wife looking like that. You'd have to tell her what happened, and she'll always worry about you when you're on duty.'

Wisting descended to the changing room, where he stripped and took a hot shower. A scab had already formed on the cut and it now looked like nothing more than a scratch. He dropped his wet clothes into a rubbish bag before putting on the jogging gear he had left in his locker. Now clean and dry, he called in at the duty desk, updated them on what had happened, and took a cup of coffee and a roll of police tape out to his car.

It had grown dark by the time he returned to the barn. He no longer had a flashlight, but worked in the light from his car headlamps. Once he had cordoned off the area, he went back to see Knut Heian.

The tractor was gone, and it was his wife who answered the door. He avoided going into details about what had taken place, and simply told her that the barn had collapsed under the weight of snow and the area had been sealed off until the police could check it out the following day.

Ingrid was sitting in the living room, reading, when he arrived home. Line and Thomas lay on a blanket on the floor and he lay down beside them, letting Thomas grab hold of his

116

index finger. He had his mother's eyes. They both had. Bright, pale-blue eyes.

'Have you been to the gym?' Ingrid asked.

'I had to change.' He told her about the skeleton and the barn that had caved in, but said nothing about being trapped for more than an hour.

Line watched him with her big blue eyes while he talked. Kneeling up, he lifted her and rubbed his unshaven chin against her soft skin. She laughed uproariously and began to explore his nose with her tiny fingers.

'I wonder what will become of her,' Ingrid chuckled. 'She's so inquisitive.'

'Maybe she'll become a researcher,' Wisting said. 'Or an investigator?'

'She can be anything she wants to be.'

Arms outstretched, Wisting held his daughter in front of him. She was at the very beginning of life and no matter what direction she eventually wanted to take, he knew he would follow her willingly.

He laid her down and hoisted Thomas up. He was determined not to treat either of them differently, but it was easier with Line, he had to admit, because she was so responsive. She kicked about, laughed and waved her arms. Thomas was quieter. There was nothing wrong with that of course – they were just different.

He carried his son across to the settee and sat with him on his knee. 'I need the car tomorrow. Is that okay?'

'If you do some shopping before you come home. There's a list in the kitchen.'

After an hour or so chatting to Ingrid, he changed the twins and put them to bed, sat at the typewriter he had borrowed from his father-in-law, and started his report. He was aware there were a lot of balls in the air, but he tried to summarise things as he had learned to do at Police College: easily understood, clear, serious and matter-of-fact, and in chronological order. It was past midnight by the time he had written a satisfactory version.

Ingrid had fallen asleep. He checked on the twins before he undressed and lay down beside her. One of the last things that passed through his mind was how many sleepless nights this job was going to give him.

24

Wisting arrived early at the police station, while Dokken was chairing the morning meeting of section leaders and local investigators.

Once again, the woman in the records office brought him a cup of coffee and smiled at him as she had before. This time he remembered her name, Bjørg Karin, and he used it when he took the cup and thanked her.

She handed him a sheet of paper. 'I thought you'd be interested in this,' she said, before returning to her desk.

It was a copy of a letter to *Norsk Lysingsblad*, the government publication with lists of job vacancies in the public sector, requesting the placement of an advert. From 1 March, there would be a vacancy for an investigator in the Criminal Investigation Department at Larvik police station. He read the description through twice before folding the paper and tucking it into his back pocket.

At quarter to nine, the door to the Chief Inspector's office opened and the team of investigators, all in shirts and ties, marched out, leaving Ove Dokken sitting at his desk with the Superintendent.

Wollert Hagen was a heavy-set man with a grey complexion and bags under his eyes. Wisting had worked at the police station for six months but had not yet formally met him.

Dokken called him in. Wollert Hagen looked up from his papers and rose slightly to shake his hand.

He sat down. 'How did things go in Oslo?' he asked Dokken.

The Chief Inspector took another cigarette out of his packet. 'Four men were arrested. They have a good case against them for a robbery in Ski and another in Mysen, so we'll see what comes of that.' He squinted as he lit his cigarette.

Wisting produced a plastic wallet from inside his notebook. He handed Dokken the three copies he had made of his report.

Behind him, the crime scene technician entered the office and closed the door.

'I asked Finn Haber to join us,' Dokken said, waving the newcomer into a chair.

Wisting spent almost an hour going through his account. Finn Haber interrupted a few times, but Wollert Hagen listened in silence.

Dokken lit yet another cigarette when he finished. 'What do you think we ought to do now?'

Wisting was unprepared. He had anticipated that he would give a report about what he had done, and that Dokken and the Superintendent would decide the way forward.

'We should get the body out and identify it,' he replied, 'and then we must speak to Anna Skaugen.'

Dokken glanced at the Superintendent.

'Agreed,' he said. 'The veteran car also needs to be removed from the barn. As I understand it, there are almost fifty years between the two incidents. The car has been there since 1925, while the body has probably lain since 1973. Nevertheless, there could be a connection, at least if this Anna the letter is addressed to is the same one who learned about the consignment of cash in 1925.'

'Shouldn't we open the letter?' Haber asked.

'Yes, I think so,' the Superintendent answered. 'Where is it?'

'I have it in my car,' Wisting replied, 'but could I make a suggestion? Anna Skaugen is possibly the only person who can provide us with answers about what happened in the barn. I was thinking of using the letter as an opening gambit. If it is in fact a farewell letter from her father, it would be more respectful for her to receive it unopened. It might be easier to get her to talk. Otherwise it could turn her against us.'

'Good thinking,' Haber commented.

'The letter has been lying in the barn for years, so we can wait a few more hours to find out about the contents,' Wisting added.

'Fine,' Dokken said, stubbing out his cigarette. 'Let's get cracking.'

25

Work had been going on at the barn for some time when Wisting arrived. A group of policemen in overalls were shovelling snow and removing the remains of the rubble, creating a broad path inside, towards the spot where the skeleton was situated.

Finn Haber stood beside his car, pouring coffee from a thermos into a cup and watching the men at their labours.

Wisting parked some distance away before approaching. The temperature had dropped as the morning progressed. Snow crunched under his boots and his breath trailed as a white cloud.

Haber took out another cup and handed it to him. 'I've tried to cast my mind back,' he said, as he poured the coffee. 'I was here in 1973.'

'Here?'

'Not exactly here,' Haber admitted with a smile, pointing the hand holding the coffee cup towards the collapsed building. 'I had been working in Oslo for a couple of years and came here in the spring of 1973. Not as a technician, I didn't go in for that until later. I worked with the dog patrol and was posted here. I've tried to recall whether anyone was reported missing that summer.'

Haber broke off and took a mouthful of coffee. 'And I've got a good memory,' he added, tapping his forehead with one finger. 'There wasn't.'

'Are you certain?'

Haber nodded. 'There would have been a fuss. If a man were reported missing a search would have been organised and I would have been called out with Jack, my dog. Then the disappearance would have moved into an investigative phase. It would have been an unsolved case that haunted the department for weeks and months to come. I would remember a case like that.'

Wisting glanced across at the digging men. 'Maybe he was never reported missing? Or maybe we've got the year wrong?'

One of the men in overalls raised his hand and shouted. Haber tossed the rest of his coffee on the snow. 'Well,' he said, screwing the lid back on the thermos flask. 'It's that sort of thing we're here to find out.'

Wisting knew he should have investigated more thoroughly before presenting his report. Bjørg Karin had access to all the old records. It would probably have been an easy job for her to look up a missing person case from 1973. Information about whether anyone had been reported missing in the relevant period ought to have been included in his report.

His coffee had gone cold. He put it down and followed Haber into what was left of the old barn.

His colleagues from the uniformed branch stood resting on their shovels. They had reached the horse-drawn carriage. The top layer of snow had been removed, and they had taken away the hood and other parts of the vehicle. A bone was poking out of the snow.

'Okay,' Haber said, setting down his case. 'Take a break.'

The men went off to have a coffee break. Haber took out a small spade and began to work around the bone protruding from the snow. Eventually other fragments were uncovered, and he stood back to take a photograph before collecting them in a plastic container.

Wisting watched as the cold penetrated the soles of his boots. He had thought that the crime scene technician's work would be more laborious, but he was quick and efficient. Twenty minutes later, he had dug his way through to the gun.

'You were right. It's a Luger.'

He pulled it out of the snow, clicked on the safety catch,

123

and dropped it into an evidence bag. In the same way, he jiggled loose the wristwatch and the leather belt, which was still intact.

Wisting took the bag, held it up and scrutinised the watch through the plastic. It was an ordinary Seiko model, with no engraving.

Two of the overalled policemen began to dig where Wisting had said the rucksack was located. The others began to clear a path to the vintage car.

Haber found the skull and took out a little brush to sweep away the snow around it.

'How long do you think it's been here?' Wisting asked.

'Difficult to say. There are too many variables. It could well be ten years, but it could also be twenty.'

Wisting turned when he heard a car approach. It drove all the way up to the crime scene tape before drawing to a halt. Ove Dokken alighted and zipped up his jacket before joining them. He grunted something about how cold it was before producing a packet of cigarettes and fishing out a smoke. He was about to put the packet back, but changed his mind and offered Wisting one. Wisting shook his head.

Straightening up, Haber grabbed the camera and pictured the skull from various angles.

'Who is it?' Dokken asked, blowing smoke on the fragments of bone.

Wisting turned his gaze to the men searching for the ruck-sack.

'Best guess is Alfred Danielsen. At least, it's his rucksack that was lying here.'

'It's not him,' Dokken said, pushing his hands into his jacket pockets. 'Alfred Danielsen is lying in Tanum churchyard. He died in 1968. I knew him. Caught him red-handed when he tried to break open the municipal treasurer's strongbox some-time in the fifties.'

Wisting let the information sink in. 'Have you spoken to

Bjørg Karin? Was anyone reported missing in the relevant period?'

'No. That's why I asked. Who is it?'

Haber lifted the skull and placed it in a separate cardboard box. The cranium had numerous fractures in every direction from a cleft at the back of the head. Wisting harboured some thoughts about who it might be, but chose not to share them.

Haber went on gathering the bones. Dokken pinched his cigarette between two fingers. 'Do you still have the letter in your car?' he asked, returning the half-smoked cigarette to the packet.

Wisting nodded.

Dokken thrust his hands into his pockets again and hunched his shoulders. 'You need to get a move on.'

26

Wisting phoned the Population Register offices for her address. Anna Skaugen lived in Bugges gate in Torstrand. Born in 1907, she had been listed as a widow since 1 January 1979.

Icicles hung from the eaves of the two-storey building. Several of the asbestos cement tiles on the exterior cladding had loosened and hung askew. The windows were grey with dust and bird droppings, and it was impossible to see either in or out.

He parked in front of a dilapidated garage. Two mailboxes on the fence by the pavement were almost buried in snow. The name Anna Skaugen was written on the lid of one and a narrow, well-trodden path led to the steps. He followed the tracks and saw two doorbells: Jens Brun and Anna Skaugen. He pressed the lower of these.

Nothing about the plump, elderly woman who opened the door reminded him of the eighteen-year-old, smiling girl he had seen in the photograph at Ruth Skaugen's home. Her hair was silver, and the curls were gone. A large liver spot had formed on her forehead, and deep furrows ran from her nose down to the corners of her mouth. Beneath her chin, a fold of skin made her mouth look even weaker. She was seventy-six, but looked older.

'Anna Skaugen?'.

She cocked her head, as if her hearing was weak. 'Who is asking?'

He gave his name. 'I'm from the police.' He raised his voice. 'I've brought a letter that I believe may be addressed to you.'

'A letter?'

'I need to explain,' he said. 'May I come in?'

She looked at him for a few moments. In the end she shivered and took a step back, as if the cold had forced her to let him enter.

He followed her into the hallway, past the staircase leading to the upper floor and a telephone table, through a half-open door until he stood in a small living room with closed curtains. It was dark and smelled nauseatingly of dusty, dead air and potted plants with damp earth.

A door opened elsewhere in the house. 'Who is it?' called a male voice. She turned to face the staircase in the hallway. 'It's for me!' she replied. 'My grandson,' she told Wisting. 'He doesn't have a job.'

Walking towards a three-piece suite, she took hold of the backrest on one chair, and stood until Wisting had sat down.

He placed his notebook on the coffee table and waited until she was also seated. Music boomed from the floor above: loud, insistent vibrations.

'I'm afraid I've come with bad news,' Wisting began, explaining that they had found a dead man in a barn at the entrance to Tveidalen.

She listened intently.

'The barn has been more or less unused since the mid-fifties,' he said. 'The man we've found has probably been lying there for a long time, and not been discovered until now.'

She nodded, as if she had added up the information in her head and had managed to get it to tally.

'Inside the barn, we also found a rucksack. There was a name written on it: Alfred Danielsen.'

She gasped for breath and was overcome by a fit of coughing. 'My father,' she said. 'Alfred Danielsen was my father.'

He wanted to ask whether she knew whose skeleton could have ended up in the barn, but restrained himself. The questions could wait.

'There was a letter inside the rucksack,' he said, and drew the envelope from his notebook.

Anna Skaugen glanced at it. 'From Kai?' she asked in a voice that had grown unsteady.

He did not understand. The Population Register said she had become a widow when Kai Skaugen died on 1 January 1979, and he wondered whether she had perhaps become senile, that her memory was failing her and she was not entirely abreast of current events.

'We haven't opened it,' he said, pushing the yellowed envelope across to her.

She sat gazing at it before picking it up, dropping her hands to her lap to conceal a slight tremor.

'I can fetch a knife,' he offered, so that she did not have to rip the envelope open. He got to his feet and headed into the kitchen, where washing up was drying on a dishtowel on the worktop. He brought a butter knife back to the living room.

'Would you like me to do it?' he asked, holding up the knife.

She did not reply, but took the knife and slowly cut the envelope open. He took it back when she was finished, and sat down again. He would have preferred to leave her alone, but this was now a police matter.

The letter lay in her hands. Her eyes had become distant. He had no wish to rush her.

'Tell me about Kai,' he asked after some time had elapsed.

Anna Skaugen cleared her throat. 'He disappeared.'

He leafed through his notes. 'But he died on 1 January 1979.'

She shook her head. 'That was simply to bring things to a conclusion. By then he had been missing for ten years. They never found him, but everyone assumed he was dead and they had to get everything sorted for the records and the system. "Presumed dead" is how they worded it in the papers. Then they decided on a date.'

Fresh possibilities opened. Everything might well hang together in a different way from what he had first thought.

Anna Skaugen withdrew the dry sheets of paper from the envelope. The music above them was turned up even louder, and water began to gush through the pipes.

She read in silence. Blinking away a few tears, she put the first sheet behind the other and read on.

'Thank you,' she almost whispered when she had finished. 'It's from Kai.'

He paused, waiting, but nothing more came. 'What does he write?' he asked.

'It's from 1973.' She returned to the first sheet. 'He wrote it on 25 July 1973.' Swallowing, she folded the sheets together. 'He says he can't go on. That summer is ending and he doesn't want to go into the dark time again.' Anna Skaugen sat with the letter on her knee, as if trying to hold on to her husband. 'Can I keep it?'

'Sorry, but I have to take it with me. I need a copy,' he told her, 'but you'll get it back again. It's your letter.'

'Where did you find him?'

He repeated what he had told her about the barn. 'It looked as though he'd been living there for a while.'

'He was in Oslo,' Anna Skaugen explained. 'That was where he usually went, with no fixed abode. He loafed around and spent the nights in that kind of place.'

'Did you tell the police he was missing?'

'Not at once. He was often away for lengthy periods. Sometimes I heard from people who had seen him. One summer somebody thought they had met him in the railway station here in town. It might have been that year, in 1973. I thought he would come home, but I never saw him again.'

She explained how difficult life had been with her husband. He had experienced periodic bouts of depression and had continually sailed close to the wind. He had been in prison on a number of occasions. The first time was in 1927, when she had given birth to their first child.

He remembered how Ruth Skaugen and her husband had broken off contact with Anna and Kai. Now he could see why. In conversation with Ruth Skaugen she had not mentioned anything about how her brother-in-law had gone missing, just said he was deceased, and busied herself with the *lefse* and the coffee pot and continued the conversation. What he learned now, he could have found out the day before if he had framed his questions the way an experienced investigator would probably have done.

'How did he die?' Anna Skaugen asked abruptly. 'Do you know?'

The question took him by surprise. He was ill prepared for going into detail about the death. 'We found a pistol,' he said carefully.

The old woman shivered. 'Ugh, that dreadful pistol.'

The phone rang in the hallway and the music on the upper floor was turned down. He heard hurried footsteps on the stairs. 'I'll get it!' her grandson shouted, and closed their door.

As they waited impatiently for him to finish, Anna Skaugen fidgeted with the letter. It sounded as though her grandson was trying to keep his voice lowered. After a minute or so he climbed the stairs again.

'We found something else in the barn,' Wisting went on. 'There was an old car in there, hidden underneath a tarpaulin. It belonged to the brothers Marvin and Martinius Bergan who ran a haulage company in Oslo in the twenties. The car and its driver went missing during a delivery of cash in 1925.'

Anna Skaugen rose remarkably easily from her chair, and crossed the room to a sideboard and a collection of family photographs on the wall.

'Do you know anything about it?' he asked.

'Of course,' she answered. 'The man who disappeared was related to Ruth, who was married to Kai's brother. He was with them, and with the car, a few days before he went missing.'

'You were there too?'

'It's so long ago,' she said, shaking her head.

'It concerns a criminal case.' Wisting prepared to conduct the rest of their conversation along more formal lines.

'I spoke to the police at that time,' she said. 'I remembered more then than I do now, but there was nothing to tell, really. I knew nothing. That's how it still is.'

She turned to the wall again, unhooked a photograph and brought it across to the coffee table. 'There's Kai,' she said, handing him the framed picture.

It was old. To judge from his age, it looked as if it had been taken some time before the war. He was wearing a suit with a waistcoat, white shirt and tie.

'I talked to Ruth yesterday,' Wisting said, putting down the picture. 'Your sister-in-law.'

Anna Skaugen resumed her seat.

'She told me something different. She said that Marvin Bergan was going to Kristiansand to pick up a consignment of money, but that she and all of you had omitted to tell the police because the assignment was secret and he should not have said anything about it. Is that correct?'

'It's so long ago.'

'Did you know that he was to pick up money?'

'Probably,' she said. 'We didn't mention it to the police, because we shouldn't really have known anything about it.'

He sat upright. 'Whose suggestion was it to leave out that information?'

Anna Skaugen shook her head dejectedly. 'That was just how things turned out. We let it lie.'

'You must have come to some agreement in advance, surely? You can't all simply have thought the same thought. Someone must have taken the initiative.'

'Does it matter?'

He did not want to tell her that whoever had put forward the suggestion could be the robber and had everything to gain by their silence. Instead he gave her time to think.

'It must have been Ruth or Dagfinn,' she said. 'After all, he was their cousin. They would most likely have wanted to protect him.'

'How did you get to know that Marvin and the consignment of cash were missing?'

'Kai told me one day. He had been at Dagfinn's to finish working on the new hayloft.'

'Kai was at his brother's every day that week?'

She said yes.

'What, apart from that, did he do on those days?'

'Not much ... nothing I can remember, anyway. We weren't living together at that time, so I didn't see him every day.'

Wisting glanced down at the framed photograph of Kai Skaugen. Of the group gathered around the table at Brekke Farm in August 1925, he was the number one candidate to have been behind the robbery. His life was not well ordered at that time, and never came to be in the years that followed. If he had had anything to do with what had happened the woman facing him must know about it, or at least have some idea.

He raised his eyes. He did not have enough experience to be sure whether a person was lying or telling the truth, but he thought he could discern a slight twitch around her right eye. A nerve that caused the muscle to move involuntarily, as a sign of something she was hiding. If not, then it was simply a twitch caused by her advanced age.

He asked a few further questions about what Kai Skaugen had done on the day the robbery had taken place, and about his finances, balancing on the edge of accusation. He got nowhere.

They heard a noise on the stairs again. The grandson popped his head round the living room door. His hair was damp and he was wearing a black leather jacket. His gaze lingered for a moment on Wisting before shifting to his grandmother. 'I'm heading out.'

The old woman nodded, and the grandson took his leave.

Wisting stood up. He could not make further progress. 'Have you ever met Ragna Bergan?' he asked.

'Who's that?'

'I spoke to her before the weekend,' he said. 'She was married to the brother of Marvin, the driver. She's been like you since 1925, with no answers.'

The old woman's eyes changed. He did not know if he

had sowed the seeds of something he could steer forward but, before anything came of it, they were interrupted by the grandson.

'You'll have to move your car. If you're the owner of the Volvo. It's parked in front of the garage.'

'Sorry,' Wisting said.

Anna Skaugen got up stiffly. Taking her hand, Wisting thanked her for seeing him and turned towards the door.

'The envelope,' he remembered just in time. 'I really must take it with me. You'll get it back again.'

She peered in bewilderment at the envelope still lying on the chair. 'Of course,' she said, and picked it up for him.

He thanked her again.

The grandson stood on the pavement going through the post in the mailbox. When Wisting emerged, he put it all back and moved towards the garage. Wisting got into his car and drove forward a short distance. In his rear-view mirror, he saw a car reverse out of the garage. He waited until it had left, and opened the envelope to read the letter.

There had been two sheets of paper, he was sure of that. Now there was only one. The other must be inside with Anna Skaugen. The letter he held opened with the words *Dear Anna*, and was signed *Your Kai*. A complete letter, but all the same he was certain that she had pulled out two sheets.

He put the letter back and felt the envelope. It seemed thinner than it had done before it was opened.

He retraced his steps and rang the doorbell. Anna Skaugen came to the door, now wearing a knitted woollen jacket.

'I think I left one of the sheets of paper from the envelope,' he said.

The old woman shook her head. 'There was only one sheet.'

'I'm pretty certain there were two. Can I come in and look? Maybe it slipped to the floor.'

She moved aside and let him pass.

He lifted the cushion on the chair where the old woman

133

had been sitting, and moved the framed photograph of her husband, but found no trace of the missing sheet.

'There was only one,' she repeated.

Wisting studied her. The twitch in her right eye was back. He was sure she was lying.

27

Ove Dokken was far from pleased, having read through the report of the meeting with Anna Skaugen. Finn Haber was seated on the settee by the window in his office. Wisting sat on a wooden chair intended for visitors.

Wisting was still certain that there had been two sheets of paper in the envelope, but had omitted any mention in his report. Instead he had given a verbal account of that detail.

'I think she's hiding something,' he said.

'It's no use thinking that,' Dokken snapped, lifting the copy of the letter. 'It tells us nothing. There's nothing of any interest here. Just that he's depressed. It doesn't even say that he intends to kill himself, only that life is difficult.'

'She should never have been given the letter,' Haber said. 'We need a definite ID. Kai Skaugen still features in the finger-print records, even though he's dead. We could have checked the prints against the letter.'

That thought had never even entered Wisting's head.

'Is it too late?'

'Maybe not, but to be honest, it was unnecessary to meddle.' The crime scene technician leaned forward. 'Did you ask her if she had anything handwritten by her husband? Something with his signature that we could use to compare with the letter?'

'No.'

'What about the watch?' Dokken asked. 'Did you ask whether she could recognise the watch we found?'

Wisting shook his head. He had not thought of that either.

'Even better,' Haber said, 'did she have a photo of him wearing the watch?'

'She showed me a picture.'

'Was he wearing a watch?'

'I didn't notice.'

'What about her father's rucksack?' Dokken continued. 'Did she confirm that her husband used it? Had he commandeered it when his father-in-law died or something?'

'We didn't go into that.' Wisting said apologetically.

'The pistol, then?' Dokken blew out smoke. 'Did she know whether her husband had a Luger?'

'It appeared so.'

'But you didn't ask her?'

'I can phone and ask for further information,' Wisting suggested.

'Do that.' Dokken pushed the report across the desk. 'Talk to her again and write a fresh account.'

Wisting took back the deficient report. 'Sorry,' he muttered, as he got to his feet.

'I shouldn't have sent you there on your own,' Dokken sighed. 'You should have had an experienced investigator with you. Then she wouldn't have been able to trick you about that sheet of paper.'

Wisting made for the door.

'Ask her whether her husband ever broke his arm,' Haber added. 'The left forearm on the body in the barn shows traces of a pretty nasty fracture.'

Wisting subsided into the chair at the desk in his borrowed office. His meeting with Anna Skaugen would not exactly benefit his application for the vacant post in the Criminal Investigation Department.

He found a pencil and jotted down all the supplementary questions he needed to ask, lifted the receiver and dialled the number.

It was the grandson who answered. 'It's Jens,' he said. 'Jens Brun.'

Although his voice was brisk, it was difficult to make out

136

whether the parody of James Bond was deliberate, or whether the introduction had just turned out that way.

Wisting identified himself but did not add that he was calling from the police. 'Could I speak to Anna Skaugen, please?'

It took some time for her to come to the phone.

'I have a few extra questions,' he explained.

'I see.'

'Do you know if your husband ever broke his arm?'

'Yes, at some time in the mid-sixties. He fell off a ladder. Why do you ask?'

Wisting explained that this was with a view to identifying the body they had found in the barn. 'Do you remember whether it was his right or left arm?'

Anna Skaugen had to give this some thought. 'The left,' she said.

Wisting pressed on. 'We've found a wristwatch. Do you remember what kind of watch Kai wore?'

'It was pale brown, or copper coloured. Some sort of Japanese make that he didn't need to wind.'

'It was battery operated?'

'No, it was some kind of modern watch that wound itself just by the movements of your arm.'

He made a note.

'You showed me a photograph,' he continued. 'Is he wearing the watch in that?'

'I'll have to go and look.' She put down the receiver and Wisting waited. His thoughts went walkabout and, without knowing why, he wrote down the name *Brun* in his notebook before Anna Skaugen returned to the phone.

'It's impossible to see,' she answered. 'Not in that picture.'

Wisting pulled himself together to concentrate on the list of additional questions. When he had gone through them all, he changed the subject. 'Was that your grandson who answered the phone?'

'Yes, why do you want to know?'

'His name is Brun?'

'My daughter's married name is Brun,' Anna Skaugen said. 'Things are not too good at home, so he moved in with me a few years ago. Now he's looking for his own apartment.'

Wisting flicked through to the notes he had taken about the holiday cottage where he thought the night safe raiders had taken refuge. 'Is Jens related to Vivian and Roger Brun?'

'They're his aunt and uncle,' Anna Skaugen explained. 'Roger is his father's brother.'

He returned the focus to her husband to avoid her asking why he was so interested in her grandson. 'There was a pair of boots near where your husband was found. Do you recall what size he used?'

'Forty-five,' she answered swiftly.

He was keen to wrap up the conversation, but Anna Skaugen also had questions. She had begun to think about practical things, such as what would happen to her husband's remains and what she should do about any eventual funeral. Wisting promised to find out for her.

When the conversation was over, he took out the copy he had inserted at the very back of his notebook, the note with the name and phone number that had been found inside Simon Becker's apartment. Anna Skaugen's number was 32082. He found it beside the initials *J B*. Jens Brun.

All thought of the skeleton and the old cash consignment was gone. He had found a link from the car thefts to a possible perpetrator. He carried all the papers back to Dokken's office, without considering how he would present his discovery.

'Do you remember that holiday cottage?' he asked.

Ove Dokken glanced up at him. 'What holiday cottage?'

'I wrote a memo about a holiday cottage in Tveidalen that had been used immediately after the night safe robbery.'

'We checked it out,' Dokken told him. 'It was a couple of joiners.'

'Not real joiners,' Wisting said. 'It was a nephew and his

mate who were going to renew the timber cladding on one of the walls. I've just discovered that the very same nephew is Anna and Kai Skaugen's grandson. I spoke to him when I was at her house.'

The Chief Inspector, realising there was more to come, leaned back expectantly. Wisting put down his copy of the phone list that had been found among Simon Becker's belongings, and pointed out Jens Brun's number.

'I looked at the case last time I was on night shift. I thought it strange that a local car thief would be providing vehicles for a gang of Oslo thieves.'

Dokken appeared sceptical. He looked at the cigarette packet on his desk, but let it be. 'You mean that first Kai Skaugen robbed the cash consignment from Kristiansand in 1925, and then his grandson is behind the night safe robbery?'

Wisting struggled to find further arguments, weighing up whether to tell him about the coins on the floor beneath the settee in the cottage in Tveidalen. He would also have to confess that he had let himself in.

'It seems far-fetched,' Dokken said, unable to let the cigarette packet lie untouched any longer.

'Don't you think it's worth investigating?'

Ove Dokken lit a cigarette and sat deep in thought. 'Where would you start?'

'With the car thief. Simon Becker.'

'He's not saying anything, but you can have a go. He's just been interviewed and is down in one of the holding cells waiting to be driven back to prison.'

Wisting protested, 'Shouldn't one of the expert interviewers do it?'

Dokken's reply emerged through a haze of smoke. 'The experts have tried. Now it's your turn.'

'I was the one who arrested him,' Wisting said. 'Besides, I haven't interviewed anyone before. Not like this.'

'Then it's about time,' Dokken said.

28

Wisting did his best to hide how nervous he was as he closed the door of the interview room behind him. He could sense the reluctance of the waiting man, his unease and anxiety.

'Nice to see you again,' he said, stretching out his hand.

Simon Becker accepted the handshake, but did not stand up.

'I was the one who arrested you,' Wisting said as he sat down.

The man shrugged.

Wisting fed a sheet into the typewriter and committed the formalities of time and place to paper. He turned to Simon Becker and came straight to the point.

'How do you know Jens Brun?'

Becker sat bolt upright, caught off guard.

'Who?'

'Jens Brun,' he repeated.

Simon Becker repeated the name aloud. 'He was a couple of years above me at school.'

'When did you last speak to him?'

'A long time ago.'

'What do you mean by a long time?'

'I don't remember.'

'Is a week a long time?'

Simon Becker squirmed in his chair.

'A month?' Wisting suggested.

'Something like that.'

Wisting showered him with questions. What did you talk about? Where did you meet? Were you alone? The answers that trickled back seemed fictitious. After collecting them all, he turned to the typewriter and began to write his statement. Halfway through, he was interrupted.

'I can tell you what happened,' Becker said.

Wisting turned to face him.

'I've stolen a few cars. I'm sick of being in jail. I can tell you what happened.'

One hour later, Simon Becker had confessed to five car thefts and seven car break-ins. Wisting did not doubt his admissions, but knew it was a diversionary tactic to avoid talking about Jens Brun. It had come too easily, but he had no intention of giving up.

He took out the list of items taken in evidence from Becker's home, placed it in front of him and underlined the Ball sweater, sunglasses and music cassettes.

'All of this was in a car stolen on Sunday night three weeks ago,' he said.

'That could be right. I don't remember.'

'From a black Ford Sierra.'

Simon Becker sat in stony silence.

'You may have read about it in the newspaper. It was used in the night safe raid. If you want to avoid being charged with aiding and abetting a robbery, then you'd better tell me everything you know about that car.'

Becker was at a loss. It seemed he was about to clam up, but instead he opened up. 'I don't know anything about any robbery. They said they were going to use it for spare parts. I haven't even been paid yet.'

'Who are *they*?'

'Jens Brun and his mate.'

Wisting waited for a name. In the end, it came: Geir Tangen.

As he had concealed his uncertainty when he stepped into the interview room, he disguised a triumphant smile when he returned to Dokken's office.

Dokken took the interview form and began to read. Wisting glanced at the clock, wondering anxiously whether he would let things lie until the following day, or if they would continue into the evening. It was half past five.

Suddenly he remembered that he had promised Ingrid he would go shopping before he came home. Too late now; the shops were closed. He excused himself and went back to his office as Dokken continued to read. Ingrid sounded down-hearted when she answered the phone.

'Sorry,' Wisting said. 'One thing led to another here today. I haven't managed to do any shopping.'

'You forgot the list anyway.'

'Can we manage until tomorrow?'

'I got Mum to come over. She looked after the twins while I borrowed her car.'

'So, you've done the shopping?'

'Don't think any more about it.'

He was eager to tell her about the breakthrough in the rob-bery case, but held it back. The rest of their brief conversation left him with a guilty conscience. He apologised again.

Ingrid was so patient, seldom short-tempered or angry, despite how exhausted she was, how little sleep she got, and how much the twins demanded. He shook off the dismal feeling and returned to Dokken's office.

The Chief Inspector looked up. 'How did you manage it?'

'I don't know,' Wisting replied frankly. 'I think he came to realise which side his bread was buttered.'

Ove Dokken reached out for the phone. 'Then we'll gather the troops.'

29

The group of police officers divided into two teams. All were in plain clothes. Wisting sat in the rear of the car sent to pick up Jens Brun. The tyres vibrated slightly on the surface of the snow-packed street. Christmas decorations twinkled in the shop windows.

He pointed out the house and they drove past slowly. A man walking a dog trudged by on the pavement. The ground floor was in darkness, but a light showed in two of the rooms in Jens Brun's quarters.

The driver circled the block and parked a short distance from the dull glow of the street lamps. The senior officer handed Wisting the arrest warrant.

'You take care of it,' he said, positioning one of his colleagues on the corner beside the garage, where he had a good view to the rear of the house.

Wisting approached the front steps, his breath white in the air before him. Music came from inside the house.

He rang the doorbell but nothing happened. Once more and the music was switched off. He could hear footsteps on the stairs inside. The door opened. Jens Brun was wearing a black T-shirt and tight jeans. He recognised Wisting.

'Gran's not at home,' he said. 'She's at a Christmas concert with my sister's children. She's spending the night there.'

'We've come to pick you up,' Wisting said, handing him the warrant. The police logo was prominent.

Only now did Jens Brun appreciate that Wisting was not alone. His eyes flickered as he looked around. The hand holding the paper began to shake. He was suddenly like a hunted animal.

Without warning he slammed the door shut. Wisting caught the sound of a lock being turned as he dived forward and tugged at the doorknob.

One of his detective colleagues pushed him aside and threw his shoulder at the door to no effect. The senior officer took hold of the railings and held tight as he aimed a kick at the lower edge of the lock. The door crashed open and splinters of wood exploded inwards.

Wisting followed the others upstairs. At the top, a cold draught greeted them. Through an open window came shouts from the policeman guarding the rear. The others turned and sped downstairs, but Wisting went to the window and leaned out. Jens Brun had jumped and was scrambling up from the snow, heading towards the neighbour's garden fence. The policeman guarding the rear ran after him, followed by the others.

Wisting ran downstairs, into the street and round the block, aware of the taste of blood in his mouth. As he turned the corner, he saw Jens Brun emerge from the courtyard in front of the neighbouring house. Glancing behind, Brun did not see him approach.

Wisting lowered his shoulders and launched himself, knocking them both off their feet. He flung his arm round him, trying to hold him down, but Brun kneed him in the gut, a hard and ruthless blow. The others grabbed his arms and dragged him away. One of the detectives cuffed his hands behind his back.

A patrol car was called for and, offering no further resistance, he was bundled inside and driven off.

'I know his mother,' one of the investigators said, watching the car leave. 'A fraud case a few years ago. I think she's still in prison.'

'It runs in the family,' one of his colleagues commented drily.

'The mother was almost worse,' his colleague said. 'She fought us in nothing but her dressing gown. Howling and screaming the whole time.'

Wisting brushed snow from his clothes before walking with

them back around the block where they divided into two groups. Two began to search the garage while Wisting accompanied the others to the first floor.

The apartment was a typical young man's digs: LPs displayed on the walls, comic books stacked on the bookshelves, a record collection stored in wooden crates, and clothes strewn over the floor.

'How much space does two million kroner actually take up?' one of them asked.

'That depends on what sort of notes we're talking about,' another replied.

They worked through one room without results and then tackled the bedroom. 'Maybe he's hidden the money downstairs with his grandmother?' someone suggested.

'I can go down and make a start,' Wisting said.

He descended the stairs, switching on the lights as he entered the cramped living room he had visited earlier. An empty coffee cup was still on the table where they had been sitting. The picture of her husband had been rehung on the wall. Above him he could hear heavy footfalls from the investigators as they searched for the robbery proceeds.

Something different preoccupied Wisting. He had not let go of the idea that Anna Skaugen had tricked him out of a sheet of paper from her husband's farewell letter, and he tried to reconstruct their meeting. When she had read the letter, she had got up from her chair, gone across to the wall of photographs and taken down her husband's picture. Then she sat down again in the chair. When she stood up to escort him to the door, one sheet of paper was missing.

He pulled out the top drawer in the chest of drawers beneath the pictures. It was tight and made a scraping noise. He would have noticed that if she had opened it. Nevertheless, he rummaged through it before opening the second drawer. To pull that one out, Anna Skaugen would have had to bend down. He would also have noticed that.

To be on the safe side, he investigated all the drawers. They contained curtains and tablecloths, old magazines, photo albums and bric-a-brac.

A cloth runner decorated with Christmas motifs lay on top of the chest of drawers. Wisting lifted off the pictures displayed on it and looked underneath. There was nothing to be seen.

He went back to examine the chair where Anna Skaugen had been sitting. What was most likely was that she had sneaked the sheet of paper down into one of the gaps between the cushion and the armrest. In that case, she must have removed it later and hidden it somewhere else, because there was nothing there now.

A noise at the front door startled him. He flinched, thinking that Anna Skaugen had come back unexpectedly.

'Found it!' shouted one of the investigators from the garage.

The detectives from the floor above came tramping downstairs and Wisting followed them out to the garage.

The money had not been particularly well hidden. Divided into four plastic bags stuffed into a cardboard box, it had been shoved underneath the workbench at the far end of the garage. An old blanket and random engine parts had been placed on top.

Wisting was rewarded with a pat on the shoulder, but could not share his colleagues' enthusiasm. The knowledge that the case had been solved felt liberating in many ways, but at the same time it meant that something had been put behind him, never to return. Besides, this was not his case. *His* case remained unsolved.

30

The temperature dropped even further through the night and there was frost on the kitchen window. Two robin redbreasts pecked at breadcrumbs that had frozen to the bird tray outside.

Wisting ate breakfast with Ingrid. Restless, he would have liked to be involved with the Criminal Investigation Department, but he was back on the duty roster and would not be working until the afternoon.

' ... so, are we agreed that we won't buy each other Christmas presents?' Ingrid asked.

Wisting had not caught the question. 'I know what I'm going to buy you,' he said.

Ingrid began to clear the table. 'I don't need anything, really, but when I start working again, we'll probably need two cars, especially if you go on working such irregular hours.'

'That's just for the moment,' Wisting said. 'In the spring I can cycle to work.'

'All the same I think we should save up for another car.'

He agreed she was right and went on, 'I've been thinking of applying for a post as an investigator. It'll be advertised next week.'

They both knew that he would lose the increment for working unsocial hours – evenings, nights, weekends and holidays. In reality, his income would decrease.

'If that's what you want,' she said.

'It's not certain that I'll get it,' he rushed to add, as he carried his plate to the sink and began to fill the washing-up bowl with hot water.

The morning passed slowly. He left to clear snow from the driveway and chatted to a neighbour who had ventured outside for the same reason. At midday he returned inside and saw to the twins while Ingrid went out. When she returned he was pacing the room, ill at ease. She ordered him back to the police station.

Ove Dokken was reclining in his office chair when he caught sight of Wisting. 'Bloody brilliant,' he commented, with a broad grin. 'Bloody brilliant.'

'Have they confessed?'

'Not yet, but there's no need. We've nailed the connection to the getaway car, and we've recovered the robbery proceeds. They're up the creek.'

'What about the other cases?' Wisting asked. 'In Akershus and Buskerud and Romerike?'

'Doesn't look as if there's any link, after all, apart from our boys stealing the idea from them.'

Dokken uttered another oath to express how pleased he was with the outcome. To be honest, Wisting felt he had done no more than stumble upon the information that had led them to this result.

He took out his cigarettes and offered them to Wisting before remembering that he did not smoke.

'The clues are always there,' he said, sparking his lighter. 'It's just a matter of having an alert eye. An investigation consists of many tiny pieces. You need to have a head that's screwed on the right way to spot the connections that other people think are insignificant.'

Finn Haber passed in the corridor, wearing the dark-blue nylon overalls that he often wore while working. He retraced his steps to poke his head round the door.

'Do you have a minute?' he asked Wisting. 'I have something in the basement that you ought to see.'

Dokken stood up and grabbed the jacket hanging over the back of his chair. 'I'm coming too,' he said.

Wisting followed them both downstairs.

The veteran car from the barn was now parked in the centre of the basement car park. It seemed even more dilapidated in the harsh light of the examination lamps, but was a stylish vehicle nonetheless. A radio on the workbench was playing a Christmas carol. Haber switched it off.

'You were right,' he said. 'I've found five bullet holes, but only three projectiles.'

'Five?' Wisting had only found three.

Haber pointed them out. The bullets had been removed and were lying on a metal table. '9 x 19 millimetre. The most common pistol ammunition in the world.'

'Have you examined the Luger?'

'I've conducted some test firings. The barrel leaves a number of quite distinctive marks on the bullet.'

Wisting leaned forward and squinted at the three bullets on the metal table.

'They all have the same scratches,' Haber said. 'The consignment of cash was held up with the same Luger that Kai Skaugen used to shoot himself. Together with all the rest of what we know, there's every reason to conclude that he was the one who committed the robbery.'

'Where's the skeleton?' Wisting asked.

'It's been packed up. The National Crime Team at Kripos will get some anatomy professor or other to look at it along with an archaeologist.'

'Do we know for sure that it's Kai Skaugen?'

'The hospital records confirm that he sustained an arm fracture. That's the surest lead we have. Together with the letter, the rucksack with his father-in-law's name and the fact that he is still missing, it should ensure that this pile of bones will end up in a grave marked with his name.'

'Who else could it possibly be?' Dokken asked.

Wisting had toyed with the idea that it might be Marvin Bergan, the driver of the cash delivery in 1925, but the theory was too fanciful to share.

'What about the old case?' he asked instead.

'We're wrapping it up,' Dokken replied. 'We know now what happened, and no one can be brought to justice for it. We'll tie a string round the papers and store them in the archives.'

'There are still a lot of unanswered questions,' Wisting said.

'Who is going to answer them?'

'I think Anna Skaugen knows what happened. I think she's known for many years, and what she may not have known was in that part of the farewell letter of her husband's that has gone missing.'

He still felt that it had not been wrong to let her read the letter, but it had been a mistake to trust her.

Even though it was not Ove Dokken's fault that half the letter was missing, nevertheless he did not like to be reminded.

'You're not going to get any answers out of her,' he said. 'Anyway, she has probably burned it.' He took out a cigarette and lit up. 'Let it lie. We're never going to find answers to everything. You have to carry around a few unanswered questions. You'll just have to learn to live with it.'

His cigarette smoke curled up beneath the garage roof. 'Some of them will tear and chafe at you, and give you sleepless nights. It's just something you have to get used to if you're going to be an investigator.'

Wisting looked at him. 'There's a vacant post,' he ventured tentatively.

Dokken shook his head. 'The advert's been withdrawn.' He blew cigarette smoke through his nostrils. 'I've spoken to the Chief Constable. We thought we'd offer you the post.'

33 YEARS LATER

Wisting stood in the shade of an oak tree. The ten student police officers had changed into field uniforms and boots. The day was growing late, and the sun was low on the horizon. The sky above them looked dull and hazy.

A similar sized group of regular officers from the police station had also been mustered. Some carried spades, others pickaxes. They lined up behind the ruins of the old barn at a distance of one metre from each other. Seasons had come and gone, doing their best to hide what was left of the building beneath weeds and grass. The forest loomed silently around them, and the ground was speckled with sunlight that filtered through the leaves.

Line, tense and expectant, was also present, her camera slung over her shoulder.

Wisting again read through the faded text of the letter he had received earlier that day. For thirty-three years it had been concealed behind a framed photograph, but now it provided the answer to an even older secret, a mystery more than ninety years old.

Anna Skaugen wrote about how her whole life had consisted of secrets and lies, but also contained a lifelong love, and she told of how she had lied in that snowy winter of 1983 when she hid part of her husband's last words.

She had known what her fiancé had done in 1925. The outcome had not been planned. The intention had been only to use the pistol as a threat, but Marvin Bergan had been unwilling to stop at the barricade Kai Skaugen had set up.

He had never confided the details, but the robbery and

murder of the driver had become their secret. She had accepted him for what he was and what he had done, and entered into marriage with him. The money had given them reason to look forward to a bright future, but that future had rapidly grown dark. At regular intervals, he had helped himself to the stashed money. Never so much that it would lead to suspicions from his brother or the others, but it all spiralled out of control.

He started to drink and sailed close to the wind in many other ways. Anxiety and depression followed. Eventually, it became increasingly difficult for him to help himself to the money and, when war came, there was nothing to spend it on. After the war, monetary reform was introduced. Banknotes were exchanged for ration cards, and bank deposits and securities were recorded before new banknotes were released into circulation. The remaining stolen money became worthless, and Kai Haugen's fragile hope of a bright future collapsed in tatters.

When two sharp blasts from a car horn sounded on the road they all turned towards it. A sleek and shiny veteran car was approaching. A few pointed, and a murmur of voices rose from the police officers and students.

Rupert Hansson was nearly eighty now. Doffing his driver's cap, he stretched his arm through the window and gave a cheerful wave. The old tyres crunched on the gravel.

Line raised her camera and took a few photographs. A cloud of dust rose behind the car as Wisting walked over to greet him.

'Thanks for coming,' he said, 'and for bringing the car with you.'

'I wouldn't have missed this for anything,' the old man said, clambering out to stand beside Line.

Wisting turned to the row of police personnel and repeated what they were to look for. Approximately one hundred metres into the forest, they should find a round stone, about the same size as a manhole cover, with a smaller stone placed to the north of it.

So the search began.

Wisting approached two old men who stood watching. 'Is she the one with the ponytail?' he asked the elder of the two.

Ove Dokken took the cigarette from his mouth and smiled proudly at his granddaughter. 'She's a clever girl,' the retired Chief Inspector said. 'She's going to be a good policewoman.'

Finn Haber waved away a fly. 'So, there was another page to the farewell letter?'

Wisting handed him the sheaf of papers. In the letter that Anna Skaugen had hidden away thirty-three years earlier, her husband described the place where the robbery proceeds were concealed. The money was unusable, and had probably disintegrated, he thought, but the gold was still there.

He was in no position to look after her, but if she should ever find herself in a situation where she needed it, she could pick it up.

The search chain moved through the forest. Wisting and the two retired police officers followed it with Line and Rupert Hansson. The air was alive with the noise of twigs snapping and insects buzzing.

'Eighty metres!' shouted the search leader, who was holding a tape measure.

The police searchers began to walk more slowly, lifting branches and checking under bushes.

Moving to the left flank of the search chain, Line stopped and took more photographs. She was part of the old case too, thought Wisting. She had always been fond of taking pictures, and had become an excellent photographer. Now she was working as a freelance journalist, a tough, demanding career in a competitive job market, but she had the right contacts and knew what editors were looking for. Moreover, she had a tireless love of work and bags of energy.

'Ninety metres!'

When Ove Dokken dried his neck with a handkerchief Line turned her camera lens on them. Wisting tried not to look in her direction.

155

Haber gazed back at the demolished barn. 'There must have been others who knew about it,' he said. 'The man who owned the barn, for one, must have known something about it.'

'He was paid handsomely,' Dokken said.

Wisting agreed. 'The people who knew about the robbery kept silent because of the strike. There was nothing in the newspapers. The car was left in the barn so that nobody could put two and two together.'

A large bird was scared off from the forest floor ahead of them. Flying low, it forced the nearest people in the search chain to duck.

'They should be there now,' Haber said, glancing back at the barn again.

The search party worked even more carefully. Many of them used sticks to probe the ground for stones that might lie hidden beneath the turf.

The search leader came over to report to Wisting. 'One hundred and seven metres,' he said.

'A bit farther.' Wisting stood beside Haber and Dokken while the search proceeded.

'It must be here,' Dokken said. 'No one removes stones from a forest, unless they intend to cultivate a field.'

The search leader turned to face Wisting. 'One hundred and twenty!'

Wisting beckoned him. 'Pull them back to one hundred metres and search backwards,' he suggested. 'I think we've gone past it. A hundred metres is a long distance to carry a bank chest, and distance is a difficult thing to estimate.'

At eighty-seven metres, someone called out to report a find. The others flocked around, but moved aside at Wisting's approach.

The flat stone was covered in moss and almost hidden by a wild raspberry bush. A smaller stone lay beside it, as Kai Skaugen had described, and an overgrown mound suggested that the earth had been dug out and the hole subsequently filled. This must be it.

'Should we lift it off?' the search leader asked. Wisting nodded.

One of the men stepped forward and took hold of the edge of the stone. With ease, he tilted it to one side. The ground beneath was damp and black, with tiny insects scurrying in all directions.

A spade was passed forward, and it struck something hard at the first cut. Wisting began to clear away the soil with his hands. Under several centimetres of loose earth, a rusty metal surface became visible, corroded to such an extent that earth and flakes of rust had dropped through the holes.

Soon the entire lid was uncovered. The chest was about 80 x 60 centimetres and fitted with hinges but, instead of lifting off the lid, two of the policemen began to dig it out completely from either side. Half an hour later, they lifted the whole chest out of the hole and set it down on a tarpaulin.

Wisting squatted, with soil on his hands and face where he had wiped away perspiration. Everyone who had participated in the search stood in a circle around him.

At one time the metal chest had been fitted with a padlock. Only fragments of the hasp remained after it had been broken open. Earth and rust had jammed the lid tight. He rocked it back and forth until it became increasingly loose and could be lifted.

He could hear the shutter on Line's camera; apart from that, silence.

The chest was still half-full of banknotes, discoloured by earth and in thick bundles, partly covered by the soil and pebbles that had fallen through the lid. Wisting lifted one of the bundles. The paper crumbled between his fingers, and he quickly put it back.

In a separate compartment lay items wrapped in felt fabric. Wisting picked up one, weighing it in his hand, before unwrapping the cloth to reveal a gold bar.

Someone began to clap. Behind him he heard widespread laughter and shouted hurrahs.

A stretcher was set up to carry the chest out of the forest. They used the tarpaulin to hoist it before four men each took a corner of the stretcher and carried it off. Wisting was left standing with Ove Dokken and Finn Haber.

Maren Dokken came over and hugged her grandfather. She adjusted her ponytail, produced a tin of snuff from her trouser pocket, and tucked a sachet behind her lips.

'Something doesn't add up,' she said.

Wisting lifted a spade that had been left lying in front of them.

'What are you thinking about?' her grandfather asked.

'That heap of earth,' she said, pointing at the tussocks of long grass beside the trench. 'If that was dug out to make room for the chest then something doesn't tally. It's more than double the size of the hole in the ground.'

'Hard packed earth takes on a different volume when it's dug up and turned over,' Finn Haber pointed out.

'All the same,' Maren Dokken said, 'the mound has probably bedded down now, surely, if it was dug in 1925?'

Wisting handed her the spade.

She looked at him. 'Is there something else down there?'

'There's only one way to find out.'

She glanced across at her grandfather, picked up the spade and began to dig. Some of the other students arrived to help. Tree roots had twined and twisted in all directions, hampering the digging.

'Wait!' she shouted, when they had been working for a while. She put down her spade, crouched and took hold of a mysterious scrap protruding from the ground. 'It's a blanket or something,' she said, tugging at it.

'Shouldn't someone else take over?' one of the students asked. 'Maybe a crime scene technician?'

Wisting glanced at Finn Haber. 'It's fine,' he reassured him. 'Just continue.'

It was not a blanket they had found lying under the earth,

but a black coat with buttons and a belt. Maren folded out the lapels. Splinters of bone and brown knuckles were exposed.

'Marvin Bergan,' Wisting said.

'Did you know that?' she asked.

'It was always a possibility.'

Painstakingly, the students dug their way to the head of the grave, where the remains of a chauffeur's cap with a leather peak were revealed. Underneath, they could make out the rounded contours of a skull.

Wisting let the student police officers finish the work. All necessary equipment was brought and every bone photographed and recorded on a special form before being slipped into a paper bag. The various rags of clothing, loose buttons, the remains of a wallet and a wristwatch, were all handled in similar fashion.

Ove Dokken and Finn Haber had gone home. Wisting wanted to stay until the end.

The young student police officers gradually grew more excited. Wisting envied them their eagerness and vitality, but not the assignments that lay ahead of them. Since the time when he had started in the police, many changes had taken place. He had embarked on his career in the belief that he could help to create a better world. Now he thought that in many ways he had failed. More precisely: he thought that he had been naïve. The world, and crime, was more momentous than he was. Seen from his present vantage point, things had moved in the wrong direction.

Crime nowadays was more complex than when he had set out. Organised, frontier-crossing criminals who cooperated across national and cultural affiliations were now the norm. Their crimes were more serious, their violence more brutal. There had been an increase in corruption and bribery. A combination of illegal and legal activity had evolved, and was now in the process of undermining people's confidence and security. The relative strength of the police and the threat posed by crime had been dislocated in an entirely negative direction.

He wondered what he could have done differently during the past three decades, but failed to find an answer. He also knew there was no simple answer.

It was growing dark, but someone had brought out a generator and a floodlight. Maren Dokken switched it on, pointed the lamp at the hole in the ground, and got on with the job.

For more William Wisting,
turn the page for an extract from *Dregs*.

1

The report was phoned in to the police switchboard in Tønsberg on Tuesday 22nd June at 09.32 hours. William Wisting had just left the doctor's surgery when the assignment arrived over the police radio. Now he was standing with fine-grained sand in his shoes, using his hand to shade the sunlight from his eyes, the third policeman to reach the discovery site.

Waves broke against the shore in front of him and rolled back to sea. Bare rock faces, smooth and slippery wet, sloped gently into the water on either side of the bay. Two uniformed colleagues had cordoned off the western side of the bathing beach.

This early in the morning there were only a few people around, a small group of onlookers comprising no more than twelve or thirteen people, mostly children. One of the policemen had taken aside a heavily built boy with red, bristling hair and a face full of freckles. The boy was trying to control a small black terrier on a lead with one hand, while pointing and gesticulating with the other.

Wisting let his eye rest on one of the few seagulls flying in wide, sluggish circles over the bay, as if he wanted to take a short break before filling his lungs with salt air and bringing his concentration to bear on another lengthy and demanding task.

A training shoe at the water's edge rolled backwards and forwards, looking as if it was going to be pulled out to sea each time the sand slid beneath it, only to be thrown back to shore with each new wave. Seaweed had entangled itself

1

tightly around the laces, which were still tied, and the sole had a covering of brown algae. The remains of a human foot protruded from the shoe. Shrimp fry and other small forms of sea life crawled around, catching hold wherever they could. Wisting allowed his eye to take flight again, staring at the thin, grey line separating the sea from the sky. On the misty horizon he could make out the outline of a cargo ship.

A small van drove onto the grassy plain at the back of the shore, halting beside the police patrol car. Espen Mortensen stepped out, then leaned in again to pull out a camera case. Wisting nodded in welcome to the young crime technician. Mortensen reciprocated and opened the side door of the crime scene vehicle. He brought out a spade and a white plastic tub before approaching his colleague. 'Another one?' he asked, putting down the spade on the sand.

'Another one,' Wisting confirmed, squatting beside the macabre discovery while Mortensen got his camera ready. The foot looked as if it had been torn or pulled from the rest of the body at the ankle joint, but was still held tightly by the training shoe. Tendrils of thick, leathery skin unfolded on either side. Among the grey-white mass of flesh at the bottom of the shoe he could see pale scraps of bone and part of what might be a ligament covering the heel.

Wisting had seen it all before. This was the second severed foot that had been washed up in his district recently. He stood up and glanced at the crime technician. 'They don't belong together,' he said positively. Mortensen remained standing with a lens in his hand, looking down at the shoe.

'What do you mean? I think it looks exactly the same as the first.'

'That's the problem,' Wisting nodded. 'It's a left shoe. The first one was too.' He bent over and examined the contents of the shoe once more. 'Besides, this one has a white tennis sock. The first had a black sock.'

Espen Mortensen swore and hunched over the shoe as it bobbed up and down in the waves. 'You're right,' he agreed.

2

'I think this one's a couple of sizes bigger too. That means . . .'

They both understood what this meant. The body parts were from two unknown corpses that probably were still floating on the sea.

Mortensen took several photographs from different angles before putting the camera back into its case, gripping the spade and digging into the sand beneath the shoe. A little sand, a couple of shells and some seawater flowed with it into the tub.

The policeman who had been questioning the red-haired boy approached them, quickly summing up the boy's story of how he had found the shoe while walking his dog a short time earlier. 'We're organising a search of the shore,' he said. 'The rest of the body might float to land anywhere at all. There will be lots of children here today. The Red Cross has promised to come here with a search party within an hour.'

Wisting nodded his approval. After the previous foot had been found they had searched the coastline without any result. Perhaps they would be luckier this time. A large wave rolled far up the shore, and he had to take a few steps back to avoid getting wet. When it rolled back it wiped his footsteps from the damp sand.

He drew his hand through his thick, dark hair and looked out to sea again. He had experienced a great deal in life, but this time he could feel his heart beat a bit faster.

2

The map that lay unfolded over the conference table had a red cross on the outermost southern tip of Stavernsøya island. Wisting grabbed the felt-tip pen and marked a new cross on the bay beside the south-facing ramparts of the old fortifications and shipyard buildings in the old part of Stavern.

Nils Hammer was right at his shoulder. 'Another *left* foot?' he asked doubtfully.

Wisting nodded, pulling a bundle of photographs out of an envelope and spreading them across the map. All were of the same subject, a blue training shoe with an upper made of a synthetic material, padded edges and the manufacturer's name, Scarpa Marco. On both sides the shoe was emblazoned with red, contrasting stripes, faded after the time in the seawater.

What little doubt there had been was gone. The shoe that was found out on Stavernsøya island six days before was of the same make and model as the one that was now sitting on the metal bench in Espen Mortensen's crime laboratory. As the crow flies, there was barely a kilometre between the two discovery sites.

Wisting had delegated the first investigation and not involved himself closely. The detectives' principal theory was that the foot was from a boating accident in the Skagerrak. Forensics thought that it could have been in the water for between six and ten months. The work so far had consisted of charting all persons missing from this stretch of coast over the last year. The first thought Wisting had, when shoe and foot number two turned up, was that

4

they were a pair, but then it emerged that they were both left feet.

The coffee machine had not quite finished its work. Nils Hammer impatiently filled a paper mug while it was still sputtering. 'We're no longer talking about some kind of accident, are we?' he asked.

Wisting did not answer, but was in agreement that they had to come up with new theories.

Hammer swigged the warm coffee. 'A drugs reckoning,' he suggested.

Nils Hammer was in his mid-forties, with broad shoulders, a barrel chest and dark blond hair. He worked as leader of the narcotics division, and in his view most things were connected in one way or another with drugs crime. His dark eyes gave him a sceptical expression. Often it was enough for him to stare at a suspect to extract a confession, simply to escape that intense gaze.

'It doesn't need to be something criminal,' Wisting reminded him.

Hammer sat down and put his feet on the table. 'It's criminal to cut off someone's feet, whether they are living or dead.'

The coffee machine gurgled faintly and shot out a cloud of hot steam. Wisting fetched a cup from the cupboard and helped himself. 'It might not have been cut off by force,' he suggested. 'It's not unnatural for arms and legs to get separated from a body that has been in the water for a long time.'

'And just by chance it applies to a pair of left feet, wearing the same kind of shoe?'

Wisting shrugged his shoulders. He would not convince anyone by arguing against the facts, not even himself. He sighed. The fact was, they stood on the threshold of an extensive investigation.

Torunn Borg arrived at the door of the meeting room with a pile of papers in her hands. 'Another shoe?' she enquired.

'Another left foot,' Hammer corrected.

'A couple of sizes larger than the first one,' explained Wisting. 'But the same make.'

'A Scarpa Marco,' Torunn Borg nodded and sat down. 'A training shoe with laces,' she continued, leafing through the papers.

Wisting sat beside her. Professionally skilful, efficient and motivated, Torunn Borg was one of the most competent investigators in the section. She had been given the task of tracing the shoe type. 'Have you discovered anything?' he asked.

'It's produced in China.' Torunn Borg put down copies of order and production lists. '*Europris* imports around 15,000 pairs a year. Since 2005 they have sold just over 50,000 of them throughout the country.'

Wisting's telephone rang. Checking the display he saw that it was Suzanne. He switched the phone to silent and cancelled the call. She would want to talk about his doctor's appointment.

'The first shoe was size 43. 7,400 pairs of them have been sold.'

'That certainly makes it easier,' Hammer commented drily, biting into his paper mug. 'Who actually buys training shoes at *Europris*?'

'Sports shoes,' Torunn corrected him and held out a brochure that explained the shoe was made of artificial leather and had a moulded sole of ethylene-vinyl-acetate, which offered good shock absorption.

'Old people.' Wisting replied. 'My father shops at *Europris*. It's reasonably priced, and he's happy with the quality. The feet must belong to two of *The Old Folk*.'

The two others fell silent, knowing he was right.

The list of missing people during the past year was not a long one. It contained only four names. Wisting had them in front of him.

Torkel Lauritzen

Otto Saga

Sverre Lund

Hanne Richter

All four had disappeared within the space of a few days in September of the previous year.

The cases had caused a headache. Each year around fifty people were reported missing in the police district, but most were quickly located: teenagers who ran away from home, children who forgot the time and place, dementia sufferers who got into trouble, the mentally ill, berry-pickers and hunters. Usually these cases ended with happy reunions, although sometimes the missing persons were found as victims of an accident or with a farewell note. Only in a few exceptional cases did anyone disappear completely and without trace.

The first three names on the list were described by the division only as *The Old Folk*. Two of them lived in sheltered housing flats at Stavern nursing home in Brunla-veien. The third man was of the same age but still active enough to live at home in Johan Ohlsensgate in the middle of Stavern. Besides, his wife was still living.

The media had not been tempted to speculate about a connection, although they must surely have thought the same as the police.

Statistically speaking, these disappearance cases were practically impossible. There were about 6,000 permanent residents in Stavern. Barely four per cent of them were over 75 years of age and yet in the course of one and the same week, three had vanished.

The police had looked for connections and patterns in addition to age and residential similarities, but only dis-covered that the children of two of the missing were married to each other.

Torkel Lauritzen was a widower who had been head of human resources in the *Treschow-Fritzøe* group of compa-nies. Two years earlier he had suffered a serious stroke. In

7

the photograph that accompanied the case file, the corner of his mouth hung down on one side. The illness meant that he spoke indistinctly and in monosyllables, but rehabilitation at the nursing home had enabled him to manage by himself. He had partly regained the movement of his right foot and enjoyed going on short walks along the coastal path. Always precise and punctual, when he didn't come home for dinner after a walk on Monday 1st September, the staff became worried. Despite his illness he had not stopped smoking and both his blood pressure and cholesterol levels were high. They feared that he had suffered another stroke, and searched for him throughout the walking areas. He was never found, neither living nor dead...

The William Wisting Series

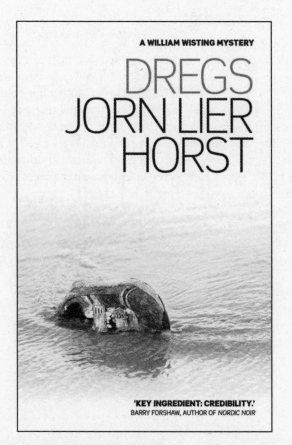

A WILLIAM WISTING MYSTERY

DREGS
JORN LIER
HORST

'KEY INGREDIENT: CREDIBILITY.'
BARRY FORSHAW, AUTHOR OF *NORDIC NOIR*

Police Inspector William Wisting has many years of experience, but he has never seen evidence like this. Four feet washed up on the beach... from four different victims?

'*Dregs* is immensely impressive. The writer's career as a police chief has supplied a key ingredient: credibility.'

Barry Forshaw

The William Wisting Series

A WILLIAM WISTING MYSTERY

CLOSED FOR WINTER

JORN LIER HORST

'UP THERE WITH THE BEST OF NORDIC CRIME WRITERS.'
MARCEL BERLINS, *THE TIMES*

WINNER - THE NORWEGIAN BOOKSELLERS AWARD

Inspector William Wisting has witnessed grotesque murders before, but this is something new. Then more corpses are discovered on the deserted archipelago, while dead birds fall from the sky...

WINNER: Norwegian Booksellers Prize 2011

'A very engrossing crime novel.'
Edinburgh Book Review

The William Wisting Series

A WILLIAM WISTING MYSTERY

THE HUNTING DOGS

JORN LIER HORST

'ONE OF THE MOST BRILLIANTLY UNDERSTATED CRIME NOVELISTS WRITING TODAY'
JOAN SMITH, *SUNDAY TIMES*

WINNER - THE GOLDEN REVOLVER TOP NORWEGIAN CRIME NOVEL 2013
WINNER - THE GLASS KEY TOP NORDIC CRIME NOVEL 2013

Years ago William Wisting closed one of Norway's most widely publicised criminal cases. Now it is discovered that evidence was planted and the wrong man convicted. It is Wisting's turn to be hunted.

WINNER: *The Glass Key*
(Nordic novel 2013)
WINNER: *The Golden Revolver*
(Norwegian crime novel 2013)
WINNER: *The Martin Beck Award*
(Best crime novel in translation 2014)

The William Wisting Series

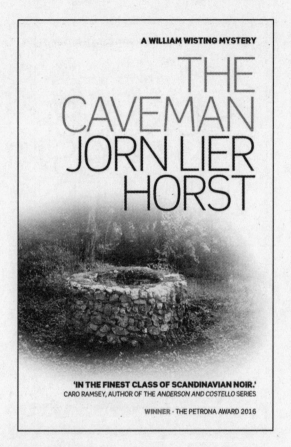

A WILLIAM WISTING MYSTERY

THE CAVEMAN

JORN LIER HORST

'IN THE FINEST CLASS OF SCANDINAVIAN NOIR.'
CARO RAMSEY, AUTHOR OF THE *ANDERSON AND COSTELLO* SERIES

WINNER - THE PETRONA AWARD 2016

Only three houses away from William Wisting's home, a man has been sitting dead in front of his television set for four months.

WINNER: *The Petrona Award 2016*

'The finest class of Scandinavian noir.'
Caro Ramsay

The William Wisting Series

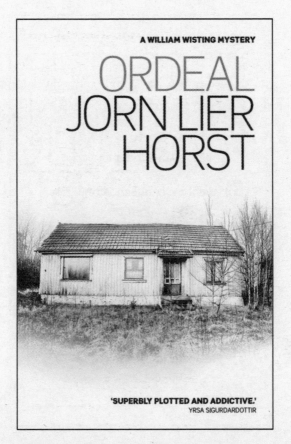

A WILLIAM WISTING MYSTERY

ORDEAL

JORN LIER HORST

'SUPERBLY PLOTTED AND ADDICTIVE.'
YRSA SIGURDARDOTTIR

This time, the only way Wisting can solve the case is to cut across important loyalties and undermine public confidence in his own police force...

'*Ordeal* kept me engaged to the end and I cannot wait for the next.'
Yrsa Sigurdardottir

www.sandstonepress.com

 facebook.com/SandstonePress/

@SandstonePress